Bloodstone

Legacy

Susan Larned Womble

Page Pond
Press

Published by Page Pond Press

Published by Page Pond Press
www.pagepondpress.com

Inquiries should be addressed to: Page Pond Press at **www.pagepondpress.com** email: pagepondpress1@gmail.com

ISBN: 0991397789

ISBN-13: 978-0-9913977-8-5

First Edition

Printed in the United States of America

DEDICATION

For my sister, Judi
My forever friend & other self
Looking forward to everything!

Bloodstone Legacy

Susan Larned Womble

Page Pond Press

Published by Page Pond Press

ACKNOWLEDGMENTS

I would like to acknowledge the support of my family, Gregg, Thomas, Amanda, Harper, my dad, Tommy, and sister, Judi. I would also like to thank my writing critique group; Hannah Mahler, Rhett DeVane, Peggy Kassess, and Donna Meredith. I would also like to thank my St. George retreat writing buddies, roomie Gina, Mary Lois, Cassie, Pat, Linda, Debbie, Sue, Amy, Roberta, Evelyna, and especially our fearless leader, Adrian Fogelin and our organizer, Perky Granger for the gifts of your talents. You are truly an inspiration. As always, a special shout out to Paula Kiger, editor extraordinaire and to Heather Whitaker for inspiring me to organize my writing.

.

Chapter 1

Homesickness gnawed at my soul and catapulted my senses into overdrive. The citrus aroma I remembered from my town invaded my lungs, impossible since it was still two hundred miles to Berry. Missed that familiar smell of oranges and the sticky, humid air of home. I couldn't wait to get there. I'd been gone way too long.

The interstate offered little in the way of visuals except for the occasional humorous sticker adorning the cars and RVs. On the bumper in front of us the sticker read, *Honk if Anything Falls Off.*

Hairs under my ponytail on the back of my neck bristled and my breath shallowed, something bad was about to happen. I was not sure how I knew, but I did.

A voice spoke to me. I didn't know where it came from, but I listened. "Beware of the arranged marriages." Hearing things now. I shook my head. Must be more tired than I thought. Besides, it was the twenty-first century. No one arranges marriages anymore.

Marriage, why would I think about marriage? I haven't been on a real date yet.

Neck hairs stood at attention again. I only had a second to take in my surroundings before I clutched the door handle. "Mom, where's that truck going?"

Mom didn't have a chance to answer before the world outside swirled—a kaleidoscope of colors. I felt strangely calm as I gripped my mother's shirt tightly with my left hand. I wasn't ready to die this close to being fifteen. I knew I should close my eyes and brace for the worst, but I couldn't.

Our SUV spiraled into a tailspin. The outside world slowed down and I could clearly see the yellow school bus on the highway across from us. I squinted and it blurred into an image of me as a five-year-old playing T-ball in my yellow team shirt. White clouds above melted into a mental picture of my sister and me hitting each other with pillows and jumping on our parents' bed. More random memories flashed in my head—opening a Christmas present, my first day of school, a kiss from my grandmother.

The white truck passed so close I felt I could touch it. I glimpsed a large muscular arm sticking out of the window. I blinked and focused. My vision sharpened as we twirled. I could clearly see markings on his arm. It could be a birthmark. It looked like a star. How strange.

We spiraled off the asphalt and onto the grassy shoulder. With a hard jolt, everything stopped. I let go of my mother's shirt. She sat unmoving, hands clenched around the steering wheel. A banging startled us both.

"You okay?" A young male in a baseball cap yelled through the window. We both glanced in the back seat to check on my twelve-year-old sister, Terra, still asleep.

"Y ... yes." My mother managed to stammer as she lowered the window. "Thanks for stopping. What happened?"

The young man waved his hands toward the highway. "A beat-up white truck came out of the woods ... out of control ... didn't look like he had any brakes, and headed toward you. You stopped so quickly you went into a spin. Good thing you did. He barely missed you. You're lucky you didn't turn over."

My dazed mother nodded.

"Your car seems all right." He surveyed the outside and peeked in the back seat. "You got a kid still asleep in the back."

"That's Terra," I mumbled.

He stared at me. "You okay girlie?"

I nodded, trying to *will* myself back into reality.

"Thanks again. Where's the truck?" My mother searched the highway, scattered with cars. A few had slowed or pulled over to investigate the commotion.

The man shook his head. "Took off. Guess he was embarrassed."

"Maybe so," My mother agreed. "Did you get a tag number or anything?"

He pulled off his cap and swiped his hand through his hair before putting the cap back on. "Too quick. Couldn't catch much."

"We're okay, so I guess we'll be on our way. Thanks again for stopping." Mom hit the window button and the glass whirred to the closed position.

The man tipped his baseball cap and trotted back to his car.

Mom turned to the back seat and surveyed my peacefully sleeping sister. A great sigh left my mother's lungs as she cautiously pulled out onto the highway.

After a few miles of quiet driving, her hands relaxed a bit on the steering wheel. "No need to tell your father. It'd worry him."

I agreed. "Okay, Grace."

My mother frowned. She hated it when I called her by her first name. I shouldn't have—she was upset enough.

"Sorry," I mumbled.

I thought about the voice. Arranged marriages—where did that come from? I won't think of it again. Sighing, I knew I wouldn't be able to forget it, but I felt calmer telling myself so anyway.

Reaching up, I tapped the star-shaped sun-catcher draped around the rearview mirror and watched the prism of colors dance around the inside of the car. "Look at it shine, Mom!"

"You know that's a present. It should be wrapped and put back in that birthday bag."

I tapped the sun-catcher again. "Do you think it's special enough?"

"Plenty special." Mom's brown eyes crinkled as she smiled.

"I haven't seen any of my friends since the beginning of the summer and—" I stopped mid-sentence after Mom cringed. I took in a deep breath before starting again. "I didn't mean it like that. Summer at the Smithsonian *was* a chance of a lifetime." I glanced apologetically at my mother. "I just missed the old crowd."

I remembered how upset I had been when my mother told me that she, my sister, and I would be spending the summer in Washington. Yet I understood why Mom had needed to get away. But, it had been a pain being separated from my friends.

Mom nodded. "Leah, I know how much you missed them, but we will be back to Berry in about—" She glanced at her watch.

"Three hours, twenty-two minutes." I finished her sentence and then added. "It's on the GPS."

Mom laughed. "So it is."

Glad to see her happy even if it was a fleeting moment. This past year had been hard. Her parents— my grandparents— had both died within months of each other. Mom was devastated. We all were.

I shifted the seatbelt so I could slouch. Pulling the side lever, I sank a little and relaxed in the SUV that served as my reminder of home, offering the smell of worn-out baseball gloves along with traces of my father's musky aftershave.

Mother peeked in the rear-view mirror. "Terra hasn't moved since we left."

I looked in the back seat at my little sister, her mouth wide open, arms flung above her, and her dark waves of hair spilling on the pillow.

"Yeah." I chuckled. "She could sleep through an earthquake."

As if on cue, a loud buzzing sound inundated my ears. Where was it coming from? A familiar sound, but so loud. I cupped my ears.

"Uh, oh." Mom dug through her oversized purse mumbling.

"What's that loud noise?" I helped pull her purse open. "What're you looking for?"

"Found it." She retrieved her vibrating cell phone. The noise stopped immediately when Mom connected the call. "Hey hon....yeah we are about three and a half hours away now....I know, I know I promised to come home in the daylight, but we were slow getting out...What's Jorden doing?...Yes, she'll be surprised....Promise I'll be extra careful...Okay see ya soon....Love you too." She ended the call and smiled at me. "Jorden and Blue have a surprise for you girls."

"Fun." Jorden was my twin. He always liked to joke about my being his little sister. He was a whole one-and-a-half minutes older. We were fourteen and more than a half, fourteen and five-sixths. I'd done the math.

I dozed off and awoke to Mother's voice. "Berry, Florida, next stop."

The smell of oranges permeated my being. I loved the smell of my town. Electrified with the smells, tastes, and sounds of Berry, I opened my eyes in time to see the "Welcome to Berry" sign— population 3,193. I'd missed that hokey sign. The number was ever changing like the lottery prize amount. I guess someone in City Hall kept up with that.

Gazing out the car window, I couldn't see much as it was dark—only a few cars at the orange-packing plant. The one red light was blinking yellow now at the only cross street in Berry. I rubbed the sleep out of my eyes and breathed in slowly. Loved that smell—home.

I only had Saturday and Sunday before school started. Saturday was going to be busy with Kelly's birthday sleep over. Exciting!

In the dark of night, Dad struggled to carry Terra's dead weight to bed after planting a quick kiss on my cheek. "See you in the morning, sweet girl, I missed you."

Making my way upstairs, I stopped first at my older brother Blue's room. No need to go in. I heard the snoring from the hall. My parents said they could not resist that name since our surname was Skye. With a name like Blue Skye, he might have been the brunt of many a joke except no one joked about Blue.

Next, I peeked into Jorden's room. We sort of favored each other. My sister, Terra had been the first to compare our hair color to Hershey's chocolate. I'd always liked that description. Jorden's rhythmic breathing made me feel whole again. Must be a twin thing.

Whap! A bed pillow hit me in the head. I saw a glimpse of Jorden running from my room.

Jumping out of bed, throwing on my robe, I ran to the door. "Come back here!" I turned to retrieve a pillow, but it was too late. He had disappeared down the corridor. I grabbed my cell instead placing it in the pocket of my robe.

"Kids!" My father's voice bellowed from the kitchen. "Quit playing and come down for breakfast!"

I skipped down the stairs following my sister and brother to the dining room. "It was Jorden's fault. He hit me with a pillow."

Mom placed a platter of bacon on the table, sat down, and laughed. "Honey, you wanted us all home. This is what you get."

"I love it, arguing and all." Dad grabbed a big bowl of scrambled eggs and put a heaping spoonful on his plate before passing it on. "Nice to be back together."

Very little talking ensued as everyone devoured their food as if we were a pack of wolves. You would have thought we hadn't had a meal in days.

I swallowed a piece of bacon and said, "There was supposed to be some sort of surprise."

"Can't believe you waited this long." Dad gulped down a last swig of orange juice, "It's in the garage."

I squealed with delight and Terra jumped up and down. There it sat. A used cobalt blue Camaro, a real beauty with stripes down the side, a present for Blue with the understanding he would be the family chauffeur. He'd spent most of the summer getting the car to work.

Blue, Jorden, and I were to attend a newly formed school with handpicked students from all over the world. The new school consisted of three grades, tenth through twelfth. Jorden and I would be sophomores, and Blue would be a senior. Terra would attend the new middle school.

As we made our way back in the house, another loud noise flooded my ears. Then it stopped.

"Somebody's phone." Mom fished hers out of her purse that was sitting on kitchen counter where she'd tossed it last night. "Not mine."

I pulled my cell out of my bathrobe pocket. "It's a text from Kelly. She and Jane will be here around one to get me. Is that all right, Mom?"

"Fine. Remember, make sure you get home first thing tomorrow so you will be rested."

That afternoon, I changed into a pink bathing suit and pulled a white eyelet sundress over it. I threw a towel, change of clothes, a few toiletries, and a T-shirt in a beach bag, then grabbed the birthday package with the tissue-wrapped sun-catcher and headed for the door when I saw Kelly's mom drive up in front of the house. "See ya tomorrow."

"Early!" Mom yelled from the kitchen.

"Promise."

I squealed when I saw my old friends and they squealed back. We rocked back and forth on my porch holding hands.

I held my hand above Jane's head. "Gosh, you've grown a foot. You're taller than either of us. You're model tall." Jane stood straighter as I tousled Kelly's hair. "I like the short cut—very cute, very stylish."

"You've changed too." Jane laughed. "Leah, you're kinda pretty—now. Not that you weren't pretty before." She dropped her head and squirmed. "A different pretty—you know what I'm talking about."

"Yeah, right." I turned red and brushed her off. It made me uncomfortable to hear compliments. I knew I wasn't pretty. I was average looking. Always had been. I was about as average as I could be. To be honest, I liked it that way.

"No, I mean it." Jane turned to Kelly. "You see it too, right?" Kelly nodded and Jane continued, "You were always cute, but now you have *it*—whatever it is."

"How?" I wrinkled my nose, held out my arms, and scanned what I could see of me. It had only been a summer. How much could I have changed?

"You grew up." Kelly hugged me hard, one of those I-haven't-seen-you-in-forever hugs. "We're all turning fifteen this year."

"Whatya mean? Y'all are already fifteen," I said. We giggled some more and dashed to Kelly's mom's car.

I scooted across the back seat. "Where are we going? I wore my bathing suit."

"Spending the night at the lake house," Kelly said. "Hey, I wore pink too." She revealed her polka-dotted swimsuit.

"I can't wait to get in the water!" I hooked my seat belt. "Is Johnny at his lake house? I noticed his motorcycle wasn't across the street. He loved that motorcycle."

Jane answered. "Johnny's family moved."

"Really? Out of town?" I asked.

"Yep." Jane squirmed in her seat.

"So, is anybody moving into his house?"

"Not sure," Kelly said before Jane could answer.

My heart jumped as we turned onto Kelly's street. The yellow clapboard gingerbread lake house always reminded me of a happy face. I had spent many summer nights on the rockers and the swing on the wrap-around porch. The car's tires made the gravel drive sing as the trees swayed to its music and Florida's humid air kissed my skin. It felt good to be back in the Sunshine State.

Kelly's mom dropped us off. "I have to go and get a few things for supper. You girls can go out to the water, but be careful. I'll be back in a bit."

Kelly dug out the hidden key from under a potted plant and opened the door, talking the whole time. We followed her into the house and quickly tossed our packs down. I fished out the tissue-paper wrapped gift.

"I got you something." I handed Kelly the package. "I picked it out special. Bought it with my own money. Happy late birthday."

Kelly opened the star-shaped sun catcher and shrieked. "I missed you, Leah." She hugged me and Jane enveloped us both. "It wasn't the same without the three musketeers."

Kelly tossed off her cover-up on the way toward the sliding glass doors. "Let's go."

We ran to the dock and jumped down to the sand surrounding the lake. The neighboring houses hugged the edges of the lake like a mother protecting her child from the outside world. Docks protruded and resembled beckoning arms built to give people a path to the blue lagoon.

I shed my flip-flops and dug my toes into the white crystals. Speedboats, skiers, sailboats, canoes, and jet skis dotted the emerald liquid oasis. The aroma of opposites, coconut oil and fish, tingled my nose. Sounds of splashing water, children giggling, boat motors humming, and birds singing proved music for my soul. My love for Florida filled my senses.

Jane untied her cover-up and pulled at the top of her bathing suit before twirling around. "Wow, this place is hopping."

Kelly grabbed a paddle leaning on the dock. "Y'all want to go out in the canoe?"

"Sure." Jane said. We walked to the edge of the lake and pushed the canoe out onto the water.

I discarded my cover up, picked up a life jacket from inside the canoe, and put it on. "Hey, I promised my mom I would be careful."

"You're right." Kelly hooked her jacket on too. "Better safe than sorry."

Jane fluffed her hair and modeled the stuffed vest, the color of orange juice when it mixed with cola. "It's such a fashion statement. Orange pumpkins are so in."

Since we only had two paddles and the other two girls had been so anxious to grab them, I sat back to enjoy watching Kelly and Jane work.

"Let's get to the middle and we'll boat around the platform." Jane pushed her paddle to the left.

Our canoe looped around.

Kelly held up her paddle. "Quit pushing opposite. We're going in circles. We need to push the same way."

A few more strokes resulted in the same circular movement. When one would change direction, the other would too. I fell on the bottom of the canoe laughing, holding my sides. Kelly and Jane couldn't help but join in. After a few minutes, we gathered ourselves.

I giggled. "Well, it was funny."

Kelly directed Jane and before long, they were making progress pushing our canoe through the water toward the middle. I leaned over and put my hand in the water like a paddle. "Now we got it."

Our paddling moved us swiftly from the side of the lake. A growing sound deafened me as we reached the middle.

"Isn't that boat obnoxious?" Kelly screamed. "I can't hear myself think. What does he think he's doing?"

The canoe began to rock. "Whoa! It won't matter what he doing if we fall in." Jane yelled. "Hold it steady!"

I held tightly to the sides. "I don't think we can. It's rocking too much." I stretched my arms and legs out as much as I could. "Maybe if we spread our weight."

Kelly copied my moves. "Not helping."

"Speed boat—" Jane grabbed the wooden edge of the canoe with her white-knuckled free hand and motioned at the boat with her other hand that was holding the paddle. "—out of control."

The boat circled our canoe full speed. We weren't the only people in trouble. Others in the water struggled to keep their boats afloat too.

"He's going to hurt someone." Kelly grabbed the side as the craft teetered. "What's that idiot trying to prove?"

"Look! That guy's going to tip." I pointed to a sailboat just as its passenger fell out. "We should go help him."

We paddled together toward the sailboat as the speed boater zoomed by in between the sailboat and us. The water grew rougher by the minute. I caught a glimpse of the thin-built driver—ordinary looking except for one thing—his bare arm had a distinctive mark that looked eerily familiar.

Kelly pulled her paddle in and huffed, low on breath. "Sailboat guy's okay. He's back in. I don't think we could help him anyway. Water's too rough."

"Maybe we ought to go back to shore." I grabbed Kelly's paddle and pushed backward. "Somebody should stop that guy. He's dangerous."

"You're right." Jane dug her paddle into the water.

"Kelly, keep an eye on the boat! We don't want him to run over us!" I yelled at Kelly. "Jane and I will paddle."

Kelly shouted. "A jet skier fell off!"

Jane screamed, "Watch out!"

Our canoe capsized. The water swallowed me. I went in headfirst. Even though I was underwater, I could hear Kelly and Jane clearly. That calmed me for a moment.

More water engulfed me. I kicked my arms and legs furiously, trying to find air. Fortunately, after a few moments, the life jacket righted me, but my hair covered my eyes. I couldn't see a thing. I reached out to try to get my bearing. After bumping a couple of times on the side of the overturned canoe, I pulled my hair to the side and found myself in the air pocket beneath the flipped boat.

"Kelly, Jane?" I coughed. I knew they were under here with me even before I heard them.

The two other girls said in unison. "Yeah, we're here."

Kelly took in a deep breath. "I was scared I couldn't find you for a minute." She touched my head with her hand. "Is that boater still driving crazy?"

"I don't know, but we need to get out from under this canoe." Jane treaded water with her chin bobbing up and down. "Let's lift it and go under the side. Maybe from the outside we can push it back over."

"Be careful. The water is still rough so the boater is probably still out there." I grabbed the edge of the canoe ready to lift.

We all three heaved. Kelly and Jane disappeared as the canoe lifted for a moment before it flipped back down. I didn't make it out.

"I'm still under the canoe. I'll try to swim out," I hollered to them from under the boat. "Then we can flip it back over."

"Okay, we'll watch for you." Jane's voice huffed out between breaths.

I shouted. "Okay." It was a struggle with the life jacket to get underwater. The jacket caught for a moment on the side of the canoe. I opened my mouth and took in water. The orange vest was a hindrance, but I wasn't about to take it off. I squirmed a few seconds, but finally broke free and emerged out of the water. I didn't see the other two girls. "Where are you?"

Kelly flopped her hand on the back of the canoe and slammed it a couple of times. "Over here. Swim over here."

I pulled myself to the canoe and held on for a second. "I'm on the other side. Stay there, I'll swim around." I moved my arms and legs. Flattening out, I took water in my mouth again. I'm usually a good swimmer, but obviously, I wasn't concentrating like I should. After a few seconds of coughing and spurting and Kelly and Jane yelling to me if I was all right, I heaved a sigh of relief as I got a rhythm going.

Completely disoriented and worn out, I closed my eyes and concentrated on swimming. A hum came from a distance. It increased in volume until it seemed to fill my head and vibrate in my bones.

Then I heard it. *The Voice.*

"Unhook your life jacket and dive under the water quickly." An eerie voice like it was the water talking to me.

I froze for a moment as my open mouth took in more water. I coughed again. I'm going to die here listening to this voice. *Unhook my life jacket?* Why would I do that? That would be the worst thing I could do. The jacket is keeping me afloat. I might drown without it.

The Voice boomed. "Unhook now or die!"

I splashed blindly and spewed out water.

"Unhook now!" *The Voice* thundered.

Chapter 2

My lungs heaved and lake water spewed from my mouth and nose as I unhooked the life jacket and dove under as far as I could. The water rumbled, engulfing and twirling me in a whirl of bubbles like the tilt-a-whirl fair ride that comes to town once a year. A roaring sound deafened me for a moment before a large shadow rocketed overhead.

I managed to fight my way back to the surface. I immediately spotted the canoe a few feet away. My breathing slowed as I watched Kelly and Jane heave themselves into the canoe and paddle toward me.

Dripping wet and out of breath, Kelly steadied the outrigger while Jane helped me climb aboard. It took a few tries before Jane was able to get me out of the water enough for me to heave myself over. I slinked over the side and flopped into the bottom of the boat.

"You could've been killed," Jane said. "Why did you go under so far?"

"How did your jacket come unhooked?" Kelly asked.

I stammered. "I don't know."

I couldn't tell them about *The Voice*. How crazy would that sound? My brain filled with logical explanations. A guardian angel? My imagination? All I knew was if I had not done what *The Voice* said I would have probably been hit in the head by that out of control speeding boat.

I shuddered, glad I wasn't dead. "Did that boat jet over me?"

"No, not the boat." Jane shivered, wringing her wet hair out. "A Jet Ski with no driver. I don't understand. It's supposed to stop if there isn't a driver. If it had hit you…" Jane scooped the life jacket out of the water and helped me put it on. "Someone's looking out for you."

Jane ended the interrogation with that comment. I could always count on her to not question, but to look for the positive. I loved that about her.

"Good karma." Kelly fastened the buckles of my jacket. "You must be living right."

Why had I recognized the mark on the speedboat driver's arm? Was it the same mark from the driver of the white truck? What did it all mean? I shook with fear and the cold.

"Good karma, I guess." I wasn't convincing myself. "Let's not tell our parents."

Reaching the shore, we pulled on our cover-ups and slipped on our sandals. It was hard to concentrate after that. I tried to join in with the jovial atmosphere. We sat on the porch while Kelly and Jane shared stories of their summer as recreation assistants.

Kelly sat on the rocking chair. "While you were having fun at the Smithsonian, Jane and I were slaving away at our jobs."

Jane interrupted, "It was fun though."

I stood. "Let's go up to your room. It's getting late—you can tell me about it on the way."

We made our way to Kelly's bedroom and all flopped on the bed.

I froze when I saw the poster on Kelly's wall. All the blood left my head. "Where did you get that?" It was a photograph of a hand with a star.

Jane answered, "That's one of the posters we got this summer from a theme park trip. I saved it because of the tattoo on her hand. It's a star formed by a snake. Creepy, huh?"

Worse than creepy. It was the same tattoo—I knew it was, and it couldn't all be a coincidence.

"I worked my butt off this summer." Kelly rolled over on the bed, oblivious to my turmoil. "It would have been more fun at the Smithsonian."

I'd looked forward to this reunion all summer. Why was I going to let a stupid tattoo spoil it? I pulled my eyes away from the wall and changed the subject. No more talk of summer. No more narrow escapes with reckless drivers. No more creepy tattoos. "Have you met any of the new people from the school?"

Jane took the bait and stood up at the dresser holding a gold earring to her earlobe as she admired her reflection in the mirror. "We went to the open house on Friday before you got in."

Kelly joined Jane at the dresser, handed Jane a box full of earrings, and added, "Yeah, there were a lot of people I'd never seen."

I questioned. "How many students are there? How many in a class? What kinds of classes?"

Kelly bounced back to the bed and clamped her hand over my mouth. "Whoa, slow down. All we know is our homerooms."

Jane dropped the earrings, joined us on the bed, pulled Kelly's hand away from my mouth, and said, "Yeah, we are all in homeroom according to our last name. I heard they're going to spend the first few weeks putting us into our *proper*—" she stuck her hand up to make air quotes "—classes."

I frowned. "You mean like red bird and blue bird reading groups?"

Kelly said, "Gosh, I hope not. What about a crow group?"

Jane giggled. "That doesn't even make sense."

"Caw! Caw!" Kelly stuck her tongue out, put her thumbs in her ears, and flapped her palms like bird wings.

We all laughed.

Kelly mumbled through her giggles, "I tried to think of a bird I wouldn't want to be."

"Maybe we'll be lucky and be in the same group," I said.

Kelly grinned. "How about the pink flamingo group?" She knocked into Jane. "We could wear pink feathers and strut our stuff."

I questioned, "Pink?" I lifted the edge of my cover up exposing my pink suit. "Not sure I could pull off this color everyday and definitely not feathers." We shared a laugh.

The rest of the afternoon, we talked about what to wear for the first day of school. Choosing the right outfit for the first day of school was about the most important decision a girl could make. By the time we decided, it was time for dinner. I was grateful for the conversation. It took my mind off *The Voice* and the tattoo.

When I returned home the next day, I noticed how messy I'd left my bedroom. Clothes, half-emptied suitcases, and a couple of bags of souvenirs including the replica moon rock an actual astronaut had gifted me littered the hardwood floor. I pulled out some of the Smithsonian posters and studied my walls trying to decide which of the latest musical groups I would retire to make room. I sighed looking around. It would take forever to get my room in shape.

A new burgundy comforter peppered with bold white and gold geometric shapes and eyelet edges lay on the cedar chest at the foot of my bed—one of those "bed in the bag" deals that had about a jillion pieces. Mom always did that, even though I told her I wanted to choose my own bedding. Maybe she did it because I always picked out really expensive stuff. I kind of liked her choice this year, although I would never tell her. My bed was an antique sleigh bed. It had been my mom's bed when she was a little girl. It even had her initials carved in the foot. I'd carved my initials next to hers.

Terra and I shared the biggest bedroom with its own bathroom. Built originally as a playroom, it was large enough to accommodate us. There was a big difference in our ages. After all, she was only twelve and I was almost fifteen. We divided it, so it gave the appearance of two different rooms. I peeked in at her canopy bed complete with new bedding—lacy and mint green.

Two bookshelves split the room. I made a place for a few of my new books. The makeshift doorway opening in the middle of our rooms between the bookshelves had been covered throughout the years by curtains of different fabrics and was now adorned by rows of glass beads. I liked the retro look.

I discarded a boy band poster with the dreamy eyed guitarist in the center and replaced it with a Smithsonian one picturing the moon and announcing the astronauts' visit to the museum. Rolling up the other new posters, I figured the complete makeover would have to wait for a later date. I'd be lucky to unpack and put on the new spread before it was time for bed.

At dinner, I noticed Dad seemed to be a little heftier, probably caused by eating out most of the summer. He had the lightest hair of us, and dark eyes, olive skin, and angular face. Age-worn now, Mom always commented on how handsome Dad had been back in the day to which he would reply—"And what am I now, chopped liver? —" and they would share a laugh.

"What's your schedule like this year?" He asked my mom.

"Eight till two Monday through Thursday. I can pick up Terra. What about you?"

Dad worked for the school system. He wasn't a teacher or a principal, but worked at the administrative offices as an assistant to the superintendent—a hectic job. "Eight to Five, but we know my days will be longer than that."

Mom nodded. "That's an understatement." She looked over at Blue. "That's why I am glad that we have Blue's Camaro to help out."

Blue frowned. "I gotta life. I can't be expected to cart the family around all of the time."

"Don't worry. You'll have a life." Dad jumped in the conversation and laughed. "Though I'm thrilled we have another driver."

Sleeping was impossible—too geared up. Funny when I'm in school I'm always hoping and waiting for the breaks and the summer. But when I'm out of school, I'm always happy when it starts again. Weird.

Thoughts of the *Voice* seeped in as I attempted to drift off. I'd been so busy I hadn't revisited the strange incident at the lake. Why was I thinking about it now? Was *The Voice* trying to communicate with me? What a crazy thought! Why had I trusted it? Was my mind playing tricks on me? Was it me talking to myself? I tried to concentrate and make *the Voice* talk to me.

Big surprise! It didn't work.

Frustrated, I flipped on my bedside lamp and went to the bathroom. I warmed a washcloth with hot water and placed it on my face, hoping it would calm me enough to forget about *The Voice* and get some sleep.

On my way back to bed, I accidently kicked the bag of rocks with the astronaut rock causing them to roll out on the floor. Sliding them one by one back into their bag. I studied the magnificent black astronaut rock closely under the light, knowing how lucky I was to own a piece of history. I knew it wasn't the real thing, but this replica was given to me by a real astronaut and I felt lucky to own it.

I rubbed my hand over its smooth texture. There was something I hadn't noticed before. Markings, some sort of an etching. It seemed familiar. It looked like a star.

Eerie!

Chapter 3

I slept fitfully that night. My mind kept replaying the day.

The next morning, my reflection with bags under my eyes stared back at me. Fortunately, the clothes I had picked out the night before sat on my cedar chest at the foot of my bed. All I had to do to get ready for school was slip them on, brush my hair, and add a little gloss.

Breakfast was just as quick as my getting ready had been. "Eat something." Mom yelled shoving a granola bar into my hand. I stuffed it in my backpack and took a swig of orange juice.

I was still swallowing when Blue jumped up from the breakfast table. "Blue's cab service is pulling out in two minutes."

Of course, I was assigned the backseat. I accepted being outnumbered, two to one. Too excited to care.

When the new school came into view, I was in awe. The beige brick school, designed by a futuristically-inclined architect, was constructed high on a hill, with the student parking lot located below. To reach the school, three sets of stairs or a long ramp for wheelchairs had to be traversed.

I climbed out from the back seat of the car. "Our school looks like a castle."

Jorden bopped me on the head. "Get your noggin out of the clouds. You're not a princess."

Uniformed adults staffing all entrances handed out pamphlets. "Here's your map. Follow the star to the homeroom list."

Again, a star?

Kelly waved in passing on her way to her assigned class. "See ya after."

Jane nodded and disappeared into her room.

A male voice asked. "Last name?"

"Skye." I answered, still searching door numbers.

"You're in 508. Even numbers are on the other side." The boy with a dazzling smile waved his hand pointing me in the right direction.

He left quickly. No chance to get his name. I walked in, grabbed the first open desk, and slid in.

Room 508 appeared to be a classroom and a science laboratory. Bunsen burners and laptops sat at every station, along with equipment kits, books, and technology gadgets that I didn't recognize. It was state of the art, expensive looking stuff.

The teacher announced from the front of the room. "Don't put your things away. We're going to sit in alphabetical order."

For the next few minutes, names were called, and we took our seats obediently in ABC order. Desks scraped across the floor as we sat, the instructor handed each of us a card with our name and what looked like a bar code embedded on it.

One student flipped his card. "What's this, a bar code? Are we grocery items now?"

Another remarked. "I don't like this. They're numbering us like we're not people."

A few other comments were quickly quieted by the instructor when he wrote in big letters across the board: QUIET!

I had knocked the bony hand of a skeleton hanging from the stand when I turned to face the front of the room.

An auburn-haired boy with a freckled nose turned around in his desk in front of me. "Friend of yours?"

I grinned at the dangling skeleton as its motion finally stopped. "No, I thought you brought him."

"Clay Raine." The boy grabbed the arm of the skeleton and extended its bony hand to me. "We're both glad to meet you."

I giggled and shook the skeleton's hand. "Glad to meet you

both. I'm Leah Skye."

His pleasant grin showed off a mouth full of braces. "I saw your name written on the list and I thought it was pronounced Lay-ah but it's Lee-ah, right?"

"No talking." The teacher tapped a ruler on his desk. "I'm Mr. Grayson, science. The sophomores will be taking—" Then he stopped a moment. "—well the whole school will be taking a series of tests for the first week."

Everyone groaned.

Mr. Grayson continued, "Your tests will be graded and you'll be put in classes according to those scores."

A girl in the front of the room raised her hand. "What kind of tests, Mr. Grayson?"

The instructor answered, "Tests to analyze your strengths. They range in length from one to three hours. We'll start on the first one after lunch."

"What are we going to do till then?" A boy in the front row blurted out.

"Raise your hand to speak." Mr. Grayson shook his finger at the boy. "We're going to go over the rules and everyone will get their identification cards. We will go in groups of five to take pictures and get your I.D.'s."

Mr. Grayson passed out huge packets to each student. I noticed the handouts had a star drawn in the corner—I thought about the star tattoo, guess this star theme would continue throughout my sophomore year.

Five students filed back in and took their seats. "Next five." A man announced at the door of 508.

Our turn. I was glad to be getting a moment to stretch.

The man at the door added, "Make sure you bring your name tags."

Clay picked his up. "The one with the bar code?"

The man nodded as Clay and I and three others followed him to an end room set up with stations, a place to register the I.D., a photo

20

area, and a desk to pick up the finished product complete with a lanyard.

"Sit. When I say green, I'm taking the picture." A woman huddled behind a camera said with a monotone of indifference.

I brushed at my hair and sat still as the camera clicked. In a few minutes, I picked up my I.D.

I shared mine with Clay. "What is this—a bar code and a magnetic strip by our pictures?"

Clay commented as we made our way back to class. "We're no longer us, we're numbers."

The next hour crawled. When Mr. Grayson announced lunchtime, I felt like I'd been sprung from prison. Kelly, Jane, and I caught up with each other in the hall.

Kelly stretched. "I thought I was going to go to sleep in there."

"I know. Me too." Jane yawned. "Let me see your picture."

For the next few moments, we studied each other's I.D. pictures commenting on our hair and picking out all of the flaws in our own images.

My stomach growled. "Where's the cafeteria?"

"Still looking for a room?"

Startled, I bumped into the boy who had helped me earlier in the hall.

He pointed us in the opposite direction. "You might need your own personal guide."

"Are you offering to lead the way?" Kelly asked in a syrupy way.

The boy grinned.

I turned all red and bopped Kelly on the arm. "Leave him alone."

I pulled Kelly away while she was still talking. "He's cute. He can show me around anytime."

We walked toward the lunchroom. The line was out the door. More than five hundred students to feed.

"I'm starving." I said as we took our place in line. "Glad the line is moving."

Kelly pointed to the front. "They're using the bar codes."

I giggled. "Guess we *are* groceries."

Gathering our salads and fruit drinks, we decided to go to the courtyard to find a place to sit and eat to avoid the lunchroom.

Blue and Jorden and their separate entourages inhabited different portions of the courtyard. Finding a comfortable place a safe distance away, I whispered to Jane and Kelly. "I bet they're going to ditch me this afternoon. I might have to walk home."

"Your brothers wouldn't make you walk, would they?" Jane asked. "They're so dreamy."

"Yuck!" I knocked my shoulder into Jane. She swayed over, fell to the ground, and tripped a blonde girl walking by with a gaggle of friends. Jane's klutzy fall hit us funny and we started laughing.

"Sorry." Jane blurted out a mumbled apology through her chuckles.

The blonde girl with a strong British accent didn't seem amused. "What are you laughing about?" She shot us a look that would kill and then turned to her group. "The girls here are so common."

"What's with her?" I asked.

We giggled again. She huffed off with her group. So much for making new friends on my first day.

Lunch lasted exactly a half an hour.

"That's the most organized my first day at lunch has ever been." Jane threw her trash in the bin as we exited toward our rooms. "Have you ever been to a school where on the first day, everyone is fed and we get to class on time?"

"State of the art school, things are gonna be different. See ya after the test." Kelly ducked into her homeroom.

"See ya." Jane disappeared into her room.

The tardy bell sounded as I walked into my homeroom and slid into my desk behind Clay, by the dangling skeleton, and in front of the empty desk that was going to belong to a student by the last name of Starre. I had read the name off the attendance sheet. Couldn't quite make out the name, but it looked as if *m* for male was written beside the name. Some boy named, something Starre, was missing. Whoever he was, he was lucky, missing all these boring tests.

Mr. Grayson passed out the booklets. It was one of those tests where you read a short essay and answer questions.

Effortless test. Hope they were all this simple. Completing the first three passages in record time made me feel confident. Wasn't one question that I didn't know immediately. I was sure about all of my answers so far. I glanced around to see if everyone else was having as easy of a time with the test.

Then I heard it again—*The Voice*.

Chapter 4

"The answer to number four has to be *B*—it works." *The Voice* said.

I looked around. No one else seemed to hear it. Everyone was concentrating on his or her papers. I went back to my test and marked another answer.

The Voice came again. "I'm not sure about question five. I think the answer is *C*."

I bit my nail. I talked to the voice in my head. *"Hello, who are you? What do you want?"* Nothing.

Why was I paying attention to this voice? This is insane. I put my head on my desk. For a while, I did nothing. I had to finish the test. Why was I listening? I decided to ignore *The Voice* and concentrate on the questions, blocking out everything else.

I was so intent on completing the test, I didn't think about *The Voice* until I finished.

Afterwards, I started to worry that I was going crazy. Was I the only one who heard *The Voice*?

As the bell rang to signal the end of the day, Clay gathered his stuff in front of me. "Get some sleep. Don't want to be dozing off during any of these *interesting* tests."

"Yeah, right." I answered with a forced smile. "Did you think they were that hard?"

Clay added, "Not really. Not this one, but we have a few more to go."

"Right, see ya tomorrow." I exited my room and caught up with

Jane and Kelly in the corridor.

Kelly crammed stuff in her backpack. "I hope we get some classes together or this is going to be *long* year."

"True." I sighed. "What's going on this afternoon? Anything?"

Jane held the door open for us to pass. "My teacher said football is the only after school activity this week. The others start later."

I frowned. "I have no ride." I pulled out my phone to call Mom.

Kelly motioned toward the school bus ramp. "Ride the bus. Look at them. It isn't even a real school bus."

She was right. The school buses were not the regular yellow color or normal shape, but were aqua and beige and looked more like tour vans.

I put my phone away. "How do you know which one to ride?"

Jane motioned to a man holding a clipboard standing out by the bus ramp. "I have to ride too. I don't have a beautiful brother to cart me around in a Camaro." She giggled as we made our way over to the guy with the list.

"Address?" he asked.

I answered, "425 Phillips."

Another uniformed man walked up. "Swipe their I.D.'s."

The first man swiped Jane's card.

"Is my address on my I.D.?" Jane asked. "204 Grenon Lane?"

He handed the card back. "Yes, your I.D. contains your address. You, bus 126."

The man nodded to me. "You, Number 629. It's right over there."

"What else is on our I.D.'s?" I asked.

"I'm not at liberty to say." He hurriedly walked off.

Kelly retrieved her bike from the rack. "Scary, no secrets anymore. Do you think it has our dress size?"

Jane and I giggled and made our way toward the buses, as Kelly took off down the street.

Jane walked beside the English girl from lunch. "I really *am* sorry about tripping you."

The English girl put her hands on her hips. "You should be more careful. I scuffed up my shoe and broke my bracelet trying to break my fall. All you could do was laugh." The three other girls in her group bunched up next to her.

I stood tall by Jane. "There's no reason to get so upset. It was an accident."

"I'm not upset. I have lots of shoes and bracelets. You girls are silly. You think you are important and you laugh at the misfortunes of others. That makes you common."

Jane's face dropped.

I grabbed Jane's arm. "C'mon Jane, they're not worth it." I looked back at the girls. "We weren't laughing at you. We were laughing at something else. You may think we're common, but you're just mean."

We walked off. Not only did I not make friends on the first day, I might have made an enemy.

"Thanks for taking up for me." Jane hugged me before skipping up the bus stairs. "See ya."

"Okay." I walked over to Bus Number 629 and stood in line.

"Hey, friend of skeletons." Clay stood a few spots in front of me. I poked my head out and gave him a princess wave before scooting back into the row of waiting students.

Making my way on the bus, I slammed into the driver's seat with my backpack as I surveyed the seated students. I noticed Clay had claimed a place next to an empty seat. A couple of people tried to sit but he said, "Taken, sorry."

After squeezing down the aisle, I arrived by Clay and his empty seat. He said, "I'm saving it for you."

I smiled and sat down. "Thanks."

The bus was at full capacity. I was glad to have a seat. I recognized the Smithsonian logo emblazoned on his backpack.

"Have you ever been?" I pointed at the logo.

"Where—on a plane?" He asked, staring at the photo on his pack. It was a picture of the Air and Space Museum.

"No, silly," I laughed. "To the Smithsonian."

"Oh, yeah." He picked it up. "I was there once on a class trip. We didn't get to see much of it. You ever been?" Not waiting for an answer, he continued. "I could spend hours or days really, looking at all of the stuff in the Smithsonian...I'm kind of a history nut." He stopped abruptly with an embarrassed expression. "You ever been?" He repeated his question.

I must have looked like I'd won the *talk-about-something-you-really-love-to-someone-who-is-very-interested-contest.* "I worked there this summer. I went every day for twelve weeks." I hoped I didn't sound pretentious.

His eyes lit up. I could tell he was impressed.

"Wow. So tell me about...well, everything." Then he added. "You're my new best friend."

Maybe riding the bus wouldn't be that bad. I told him about the time astronauts had come to talk at the Smithsonian and how I had gotten to spend the entire day with them showing them around. They had even bestowed a rare replica space rock upon me. I told a couple of space and antigravity stories they had shared with me. Clay was completely enthralled. It was obvious that he liked history as much as I did.

We'd been so involved in our conversation I almost let my bus stop pass. "This is me." I stood and stepped out into the aisle. He looked disappointed.

Clay grabbed my arm. "You'll sit here tomorrow, right?'

"In the afternoon. I ride to school with my brothers in the morning." I moved quickly out of the bus.

My cell vibrated. A text from Kelly: *bus ride?*

I texted back: *Ok*

It was more than okay. Clay was nice and we had a lot in common.

A neighbor kid was on the sidewalk as I walked by. "Hey, I lost the dial off my remote for my race car. Do you see it?"

I peeked around and saw a glimmer over near the bushes in another neighbor's yard. "There's something shiny over there."

The boy walked over and searched all around. "Where?"

I pointed. "Right there. Don't you see it?"

"No." The boy stood and let out a loud *I'm frustrated* sigh.

I walked over to the bush, reached in, and pulled out the remote dial. "See it now?"

He grabbed the gadget out of my hand. "You must have great eyes. I didn't see it and I was right here. Thanks." The boy ran off, screwing the gizmo back together.

I shook my head and headed home. The door was locked, so I used my key.

The music blared. "Mom, Terra's got her tunes up too loud." No answer. "Mom!" No answer.

I searched the house, but couldn't find anyone.

"Where's it coming from?" I mumbled to myself.

The only place left to look was Blue's room. I hated going in there. First, because you weren't supposed to go in Blue's room. Second, because it was always cluttered.

I opened the door tripping over the clothes and the shoes that were scattered all over the floor. The music got louder. I went toward the sound. I finally found it, a digital music player with earphones attached. Good thing I found it. Blue would be mad if the battery ran out. I turned it off and shut the door, and then it hit me. How had I heard that music? A digital music player with earphones shouldn't be heard.

Sounds of boxes dropping and people talking echoed loudly in my ears. A woman said, "This one goes in the upstairs room."

I searched around the house again. Still no one. I cracked open the front door. People were moving in across the street. Was I hearing people from across the street?

"Is he here?" A voice said. I froze.

Was it *The Voice*? Was I hearing *The Voice* from across the street? Or was *The Voice* inside my head?

I didn't know, but knew I needed to find out.

Chapter 5

I opened my front door wider to try to see *The Voice's* owner. I couldn't see anyone. I knew it sounded like a male. I stared and strained. I glared at boxes stacked on top of each other and spotted a notebook. It read: Zodie Starre.

Then I stopped for a moment as I realized—I was reading this from across the street. A strong feeling of fear and nausea overcame me as my stomach churned. How was I able to read those boxes?

I suddenly remembered finding the neighbor's remote knob. I crumbled onto the porch swing. My mind raced. How was this possible? What was happening to me? I thought about spidey sense. I even surveyed my arm for evidence of an insect bite. Brain tumor? I remembered a movie where a man developed unusual abilities as a brain tumor grew. Could I be sick? Shouldn't I tell someone? I trembled as tears welled in my eyes.

"Hey kiddo, what's the matter? Did something happen at school?" Mom ran to the porch with Terra. I had been so engrossed in my fear that I hadn't realized they'd arrived. Terra went inside.

"G...Grace," I stuttered, "I need to tell you something. It's..." I started to open up, but how crazy would this story sound?

"What?" My mom sat down beside me on the porch swing. "And quit calling me Grace."

I sat for a minute as my mother rubbed my head like she used to do when I was young. I needed to tell someone about what was happening to me. I knew I did. But I couldn't. It sounded too insane. "No classes yet and I don't get to see Kelly and Jane except during lunch."

Mom stood up and pulled me off the swing, smiling. "You'll get your classes soon enough. Hey, look at the bright side. No homework."

Sometimes I couldn't stand my mother, but this was not one of those times. "Mom, can I help you with anything?"

"Yeah, there're some groceries in the back seat."

I dashed to the car, glad for something to do.

After helping her, I sat by the window in my room looking across the street. Would any of the new neighbors be at school tomorrow? I remembered someone with the last name Starre was supposed to sit behind me in homeroom. Could be Zodie Starre? Who knew? I'd have to wait to find out.

I loved my window seat. It was the best part of our shared room and I got it all to myself.

After dinner, I sat down at my laptop and searched for *brain tumors* and *heightened senses*. I couldn't find much that was helpful.

I tried searching *mind reading*. There were many sites about this topic. A group of people who believed they were clairvoyant shared a test to find out if you were psychic.

Step 1: *Pick out a person whose mind you want to read.*

I chose Terra. I peeked over to her side of the room. She was sitting at her desk writing something.

Step 2: *Sit or lie comfortably and shut your eyes. Get all of your thoughts out of your mind.*

What exactly would be on the mind of a twelve-year-old? Since I was going to have to void my mind, I realized I should read the rest of the instructions first.

Step 3: *Make your mind meld with theirs. Concentrate on trying to connect your minds.*

Step 4: *If you have trouble and don't get a connection after twenty minutes, sit in close proximity. Touch the person's hand. Touch the person's head.*

Step 5: *If this does not work, then the person is blocking you from reading their mind.*

Hmmm, well they had given themselves an out if it didn't work. I had nothing else to do, so I got quiet and concentrated. I erased every thought out of my brain and tried to concentrate on Terra. Nothing. I went to her side of the room; she was still sitting at the desk.

I sat on her bed right by her. "Do you care if I sit in here a minute?"

"Nah." She mumbled, concentrating on whatever she was writing.

I relaxed on the bed for a few minutes more. Nothing.

I touched her chair. Nothing.

I felt movement and freaked. My heart stalled until I realized Terra had shifted in her chair, causing the change.

I stretched out on her bed by her chair touching her arm. I focused. I concentrated extremely hard. I took everything out of my mind. Nothingness took over.

"Leah! Leah!" Terra's voice rang out.

I experienced a tumbling sensation before I thumped onto the rug. I rubbed my eyes, saw Terra, and realized I had fallen off her bed.

Terra shook me. "You mumbled my name. Did you have a dream about me?"

"Yeah," I lied. "We were at Disney World. We were on a ride and having such a good time."

"That's weird." She pulled her book out. "That's what I was writing about. *My favorite summer place, Disney World.*" She jumped under her covers. "You need to go back to your side. I'm tired. I want to go to sleep. Night, Leah."

Talk about strange, I had lied, and my lie turned out to be exactly what she was writing about. I went back to my side of the room and crawled into bed resting my head on my pillow.

Blue, Jorden, and I made our way to school in Blue's wonderful Camaro. I felt special. I relished in the fact that we would park in the senior lot. It made me feel important. Kelly and Jane were waiting for me as I walked into the hallway.

31

"This is my favorite." Kelly twirled as she modeled a new khaki colored tailored shirt. "I guess we'll see each other at lunch after the tests."

"Ugh!" Jane groaned. "Same bat time, same bat channel."

Kelly giggled. "You always say that same thing. Quit copying what your grandma said. You need to come up with a new saying. It's a new year, and new school. Time for new things."

Jane shrugged and they both disappeared down the corridor.

I waved at the boy who had helped me yesterday. He was busy showing some new kids where they belonged. I hurried through the crowded hallway to my room anxious to meet Zodie Starre.

As I approached the classroom door, Clay grabbed me by the shoulder. "Ready for the next round of tests? I'm sure your skeleton boyfriend missed you." He winked and I managed a distracted smile.

I came in the doorway amidst a bunch of students and my eyes darted to my seat, then to the seat behind me. A bevy of boys surrounded it. I got a peek at the person assigned to the desk.

My mouth dropped open.

Chapter 6

Seated in the desk behind me was a girl.

"Hi, I'm Stella. Stella Starre." She held out her hand. Nope, not the owner of *The Voice*. Disappointment consumed me. I must have paused for too long because everyone stared at me.

Finally, I composed myself and shook her hand. "Hi. Leah Skye."

One of the boys gathered around Stella's desk commented, "Hey, now we have the sky and the stars here."

Another quipped. "Well if that's true—let's pretend it's night and we'll all go home."

The group laughed.

"No time for small talk." Mr. Grayson scolded as he handed out the next round of tests.

At lunch, Kelly met me in the hall. "I brought lunch for us."

Jane joined us about that time. "Yum, what did you bring?"

"You'll see." Kelly walked quickly out of the building and we followed her to a shady place by the auditorium. We sat on the steps and Kelly pulled out three sodas and three lunch packets, each with a ham and cheese sandwich, chips, and a chocolate chip cookie.

I nodded my approval. "Wanna share bringing lunch?"

Jane agreed and quickly added. "I'll do tomorrow's."

The British-accented girl sashayed by us. "Some people are so poor, they bring their lunch." The barb was obviously aimed at us.

"Ignore them." I said as we plopped down on the steps.

It was difficult, but I also pretended not to notice the clique's *better than you* glances shot our way. Refusing to engage them in conversation worked as they huffed off in a pack as if they were tethered together with an invisible rubber band.

We enjoyed lunch as we sat, ate, and watched people. Kelly went into an elaborate conversation about Disney World and rides. Humorous stories followed. We were falling over ourselves and laughing hysterically when Clay interrupted us.

"What's so funny?" Clay sat next to me on the step.

I was laughing too hard to talk. Kelly pointed at him and then, through no fault of his own, but just because he sat down with us, he became the focus of the laughter. Kind of like what happened with the British girl who hated us. He grabbed his stuff and huffed off.

I ran after him. "We weren't laughing at you." I let out a deep breath. "I'm sorry. Come back. I promise we'll be good."

Skepticism colored his face, but he turned around and came back to our lunch group. After an awkward few moments, Kelly and Jane calmed down. By the time lunch was over, we were all friends.

"He seems nice." Kelly knocked into my shoulder. "Potential boyfriend?"

"No," I quickly retorted. "But he is nice. Cut me a break, Kelly."

I knew I would get the twenty questions about him, but that was all right.

Our tests resumed after lunch ended. It was going to be a long week.

After school, I said my good byes to the girls and headed to the bus to look for Clay. He was already onboard and saving me a seat. I liked that. I saw Stella Starre in line in front of me.

"Is anyone sitting here?" She asked Clay. He glanced up at me.

I didn't react.

"I'm saving it for Leah," he said loudly. I smiled.

A boy in the aisle across from Clay motioned to an empty seat by him. "You can sit here. I'm L.H." Stella looked puzzled and he continued, "It stands for LeHem. I know, I know. Don't ask me, it is some sort of family name. My sister has a normal name, Beth." He motioned toward the rear of the bus. "She's sitting back there somewhere."

Stella scooted beside L.H. "Thanks."

I wiggled my backpack off my shoulders and squeezed into the seat beside Clay. "Thanks for saving me a seat. It gets kind of crowded."

"I don't want to get on the bad side of your skeleton boyfriend," he said and we chuckled.

"Do you have a boyfriend?" Stella asked, obviously eavesdropping in on our conversation.

"No." I dismissed the idea of a boyfriend with a shrug.

"I thought I was your boyfriend," Clay scooted closer to me.

"Of course," I grabbed his arm and grinned at Stella. "Clay is my boyfriend."

She furrowed her eyebrows. "Really?"

A long pause. She squirmed.

"No..." we both said at the same time then we all—including L.H. who seemed to be enjoying this whole exchange—laughed.

"We found a common interest yesterday on the bus," Clay offered.

"What?" Stella asked.

"The Smithsonian." I shifted in my seat to be able to talk to both without having to turn back and forth.

"I love the Smithsonian!" Stella squealed with delight.

From that moment our entire conversation centered on the Smithsonian. Stella had visited the famous museum a number of times when her father had taken the family on business trips to Washington. L.H. had never been so all three of us shared our experiences with him.

"What's your favorite part?" Clay inquired.

"I loved it all, but my favorite part…" Stella paused. "You're both going to think this is silly." She gazed at us for a moment, and then cleared her throat. "I know this is hokey, but I love the Wizard of Oz shoes. The ruby slippers."

I lit up. "Don't feel bad. I wouldn't admit this to many people, but I worked at the Smithsonian for twelve weeks during the summer and I went by and saw those shoes every day, There's just something…"

Stella leaned back in her seat and sighed. "Magical."

I nodded. "Exactly, magical about those shoes."

Clay quietly added, "Next time I go, I'll make a point of seeing those magical shoes." We laughed as the bus driver announced my stop.

Stella said, "My stop too." She got out with me. We waved to Clay and L.H.

"See ya tomorrow. More tests." I yelled as I made my way down the bus steps.

I stepped off the curb after Stella. "I think we're neighbors." I walked fast to catch up with her. "Didn't you move into 426 Phillips Street?"

"Yeah," Stella slowed her pace. "Yesterday."

"We live across the street." I glanced at her and waited for her to talk. Since she was quiet, I continued. "It's me, my mom and dad, my brothers, Jorden and Blue, and my little sister Terra. What about you?"

"There's me, my mom and dad, my brothers, Z and Neb…" She started.

Not being able to contain my curiosity, I interrupted, "And how old are your brothers?"

"I'm fifteen in September; Neb will be seventeen in October." She counted on her fingers.

"When in October?" I interrupted again and added. "Me and my brother are turning fifteen October 22nd."

Neb's birthday is October 26th and Z just turned sixteen. We're in tenth, eleventh, and twelfth grades."

"Wow, your parents had a baby a year."

36

"Yeah, we're pretty close in age." She shifted her backpack to her other shoulder. "But it's kinda nice being that close in age."

I asked, "Do your brothers have another way home from school?" She didn't answer right away, so I added, "My brothers stay for football practice."

An uncomfortable few seconds of silence followed. Determined to get an answer, I asked, "Are your brothers at your house?"

She stopped on the sidewalk as we had reached our destination. "No, my grandfather was here with us and helped us move in. My dad and my brothers went back with him to finish bringing some stuff from the old house. We've actually been here a couple of weeks, staying on the water in the rental cottages."

We stood on the sidewalk in front of our houses. "Those are nice places. I bet you enjoyed the lake." She nodded and I continued staring straight at her. "Hey, about your brothers—didn't they have to take the tests?"

"They're taking them at our old school and having the grades transferred here." She added, "Special privilege—so they can finish moving our stuff down."

"Oh. Guess I'll see you tomorrow in class." I turned to walk across the street.

"Yeah, I'll be there." She turned toward her house and then back again to me. "Why isn't your brother in our homeroom?"

"My brother?" I asked and circled to face her.

She paused uncomfortably long. "Aren't you twins?"

"You noticed that." I grinned. "Most people wouldn't catch it. Our parents make us go to separate homerooms. I don't know why."

She smiled. "Guess you have special privileges too."

"Guess so." I turned and walked across the street. "Stella," I yelled. "Where're you from?"

"Alaska." With that, she closed her front door behind her.

Chapter 7

Alaska. I would have never guessed that. What a change from there to Florida. I'll be sure and ask her more about it tomorrow.

With all the testing, we had not been assigned any homework. Bored, I decided to use my alone time to do another computer search about my *powers*. I found a couple of titles, went on line, and reserved them at our library branch.

One was a book about people who had moments of supernatural abilities. The little excerpt explained that some phenomenon could be caused by hormones. That made sense to me. I'd been reading about my changing hormones for a while now. The other book was entitled *How to Find Out If You Are Psychic*. Either one or both were worth a try. What did I have to lose? I'd go Friday afternoon. That'd give me all weekend to read.

Wednesday and Thursday of the first week was boring. It was tests, lunch, and more tests. Friday morning, we had our last set of assessments. The assignment was to write an essay about what you feared most. That was easy for me. I feared losing my family. It could have been because of my grandparents, both of them, on my mother's side had died so unexpectedly this year. I finished the essay with plenty of time to spare. Thank goodness, those tests were over.

At lunch, Kelly surprised us by having her mother bring us fast food: hamburgers, French fries, and cookies.

Our paper bags of food prompted our daily comment from the

British girl. "Fast food?" She snottily uttered and sauntered off with the rest of her snooty entourage. She sure didn't like us.

Realizing we wouldn't be able to keep bringing lunches every day, we decided we'd start going to the lunchroom on Monday. The British girl would probably think it was because of her. She was vain enough to think everything was about her. I guess I had to admit I didn't like her either.

That afternoon we had an assembly. Ms. Taylor, the principal, stood at the podium. "I'd like to introduce Mr. Bolcan." She continued, "He's our benefactor for Berry Academy and the very auditorium that you are sitting in will be henceforth known as Bolcan Auditorium."

A man came out from behind the stage curtain.

"That guy's huge," Clay whispered.

"That's an understatement," I murmured at the sight of the muscled up middle-aged man.

Mr. Bolcan leaned down to talk into the microphone, set way too low for him. He and Ms. Taylor tried to nudge the microphone higher, but Mr. Bolcan ended up taking it off the stand.

"Hi students, I'm Leonard Bolcan. I must say I'm enjoying your weather. Reminds me of home. I'm from Hawaii. I like the warmth." He spread his arms out wide.

"I promised you that this school would be state of the art with the latest technology. If you look around your classrooms and notice the buildings at this school, you will see that I've kept my promise. Thanks for the honor of naming the auditorium after my family. I've not only invested money in Berry Academy, but also have a personal interest in this school." He extended his hands out to the audience. "My three children—Heath, Astrid, Adrienne—are students at Berry Academy. Please stand children."

Three very athletic looking students stood. They were located in different parts of the assembly area and didn't act too happy about being singled out. They rose up and sat down so quickly that I didn't have a chance to get a good look at them. Although they were a good-looking bunch.

"The boy favors him, but the girls are gorgeous," Clay commented and then added, "Must take after their mother." He chuckled.

During the assembly, we were told to pick up our class schedules in homeroom on Monday.

"Not riding the bus today. I'm walking to the library," I told Stella and Clay. Clay looked so confused that I added. "I'm getting a personal book to read for fun."

"For fun?" Clay winced. "You're going to set too high a standard for the rest of us."

I took off down the sidewalk. "See ya Monday."

The librarian had my books saved behind the counter and I checked them out without any difficulty. I stuffed them in my backpack and started walking home.

My cell phone vibrated. It was a text from Kelly: *Made it home yet?*

I was trying to text back: *no* when someone on a skateboard glided by and knocked my arm. I caught a glimpse of him and I could have sworn he had a star tattoo on his wrist. The cell phone flew out of my hand into the street and lodged near a crack in the asphalt. Instinctively, I ran out into the street and grabbed the phone. As I leaned over, the asphalt gave way and my tennis shoe was lodged tight.

That's when I saw the truck coming towards me. I tried to move out of the middle of the street. I was stuck! I struggled to free my foot or the shoe. I pulled and tugged. Sounds of slamming brakes and a horn blaring overpowered my senses and struck fear. The truck jackknifed and turned sideways, coming right for me.

I pulled ferociously at my foot and it gave a bit. "C'mon!" I jerked my shoe as I shut my eyes and cringed, bracing myself.

Chapter 8

As my eyes tightened, I felt squeezed, and a sharp excruciating pain shot through my foot. My eyes slammed shut and my muscles squeezed. My body soared through the air and slammed hard into the pavement. I didn't feel immediate pain except my ankle. I opened my eyes slowly afraid of what I would see.

"Are you all right?" A muscular guy cushioned me in his arms.

"I..I... think so," I stammered. My world came into focus. The darkest eyes I had ever seen stared at me. "What happened?" My head collapsed into his biceps and I gazed up at him. "Who are you and where did you come from?"

"I'm Heath Bolcan. Do you think you can stand?" He lifted me as if I weighed nothing and gently put me down on the side of the road. I stood unsteadily for a minute, and then tumbled backward. He caught me and carried me to a sidewalk bench.

"You might have twisted your ankle." He kneeled beside me and rubbed my foot. "I might have caused that. Sorry. I had to pull hard to get you out of the way of the truck."

"My shoe got caught." I pointed to the pothole. Wow, I sounded like an idiot.

By this time, the truck driver had made his way to the bench and he and a few other people hovered over me.

A lady took my phone and called the number labeled "home." She paced up and down the sidewalk taking on the cell, then said to me. "Your mom is on her way."

I noticed the star on her arm. "Is that a tattoo?"

She quickly pulled the sleeve of her shirt down to cover her arm.

"Don't worry, your mother will be here soon." She handed the phone back to Heath and hurried away.

What happened after that was a blur. An emergency room doctor said I might be in shock. My ankle was bandaged and the doctor said the swelling would go down in about a week if I kept it elevated. Mom insisted on crutches. I argued that I didn't need the crutches as I could hobble on the bad ankle carefully, but when my mom makes up her mind, there's no talking her out of it. Because of her, I would attend the first week of real classes of a new school on crutches. What fun! My mom could be a real pain.

My shoe was the only real casualty. Even the truck survived with little damage. I was grateful. Since Heath had disappeared after Mom came, I would have to find him and thank him on Monday.

The doctor prescribed medication for pain. I slept the rest of Friday, Saturday, and most of Sunday. There went my weekend.

Midday Sunday, Terra sat on the edge of my bed. "I got tired of listening to your phone so I answered it. Sorry."

"You're not supposed to answer my phone!"

"I know. Feel better?"

I rolled over. "Yeah. How long was I out?"

"It's Sunday, almost two in the afternoon." She picked up my cell. "You have twenty-seven missed calls and —" she pressed some more buttons. "—fourteen text messages."

I grabbed the phone. "I'm hungry and grungy. Ask Mom if I can take a shower."

Terra left and returned in a few minutes. "Mom said fine, but said you ought to take off the bandage and maybe take a bubble bath to soak your foot. You want me to turn on the water?"

"Thanks—sorry I jumped on you."

She acknowledged the apology with a grunt and I spent the

next half an hour trying to maneuver taking a bath and getting dressed. It was difficult to do with crutches.

I went to the top of the stairs, determined to come down by myself. I laid the crutches at my feet and shoved them down the stairs while I hopped one step at a time holding on to the banister.

As I reached the bottom step and retrieved the crutches, the sweetest aroma I'd ever smelled infiltrated my soul. I couldn't put my finger on what the scent was, but I was drawn to it. I hobbled out of the doors and to the sidewalk. Where was that appealing scent coming from? Mesmerized, I had to know. It started getting closer. I closed my eyes. I breathed in; I couldn't figure out the fragrance. Food? No. Perfume? No. The smell was…

I turned around and faced the source. It was a person.

"Hi." A boy stood close. He radiated. My heart pounded and my breathing became erratic. I felt strange and my arms goose-bumped. I couldn't explain the sensation. I thought I was going to faint. It wasn't his appearance although everything about him was pleasing. His hair, his smile, the musical sound of his breath—I was transfixed. Could I stay in this moment forever?

My trance was broken as Stella ran up and hugged me. "We heard about your mishap. I'm glad you're all right." She backed off the hug. "This is my brother." She motioned toward the boy who had enchanted me. I was so drawn to him. It hit me: maybe he's *The Voice*. I wanted him to speak so I could hear him.

Instead, he leaned over and got down on one knee to tie my shoe. I didn't like people to do things for me, but this boy tying my shoe was the most romantic thing that had ever happened.

"Do you have on some sort of cologne?" I abruptly asked, then glanced away as he grinned up at me. What was his charm?

He stood up, a good six to eight inches taller than me. "I was going to ask you the same thing." He cocked an eyebrow.

I sighed. He wasn't *The Voice*.

"I don't know what you're going to think of me saying this, but you smell really good to me." I stopped.

"I probably wouldn't have said anything, but you smell really good to me too." His cheeks turned a little crimson.

I propped myself up on the crutches and attempted to block out my senses. "So which brother are you?"

"I'm Z, the middle brother. You know, the forgotten one. The one everyone ignores." He shoved his shoulder into his sister's side. I loved the sound of his voice, his look, everything about him.

"Duh, we don't ignore you." Stella stepped away. "You're too big to ignore. How could we? You're growing as we speak."

They laughed. I joined in nervously. Didn't want him to realize how attracted I was to him.

"Z's usually shy." She grabbed my arm. "Hadn't you better go back and sit down? Don't exert yourself too much. I know you've been sleeping. I tried to call you about a hundred times."

"Oh yeah." I pulled my cell phone out of my pocket. "I better call some people back."

Z said, "I'm sure we'll see each other again. We live across the street."

I listened as Z talked. Does his heart flutter like mine? I averted my eyes. I struggled to mask my feelings. I didn't want Stella or Z to see how I felt.

"Leah, come in and eat!" Mom yelled. "I know you're famished."

I reluctantly returned to the house, but I couldn't stop thinking about Z. I talked to Kelly and Jane; but all the while, I thought about Z. That night in bed, I thought about his smell, his look, and his voice. I tossed and turned and couldn't fall asleep, so I got up, hopped over to my bay window, and looked out.

I studied the sidewalk. A neighbor walked his dog. I peered down the street, startled by the brightness of lights from a passing car. All was quiet. I relaxed on the window seat, on my side with my head propped up by one arm, staring out onto the street. I flatten out my elbow and stretched out on my side the full space of the window settee. My eyes were almost closed when I saw a shadow move in the window across the street from mine. The shadow quickly disappeared. I sat up straight. Could it be?

44

My phone vibrated.

A text. I didn't recognize the number.

It read: *I c u—got u # from sis—Z*

My heart leaped. I wrote back: *can't sleep—u?*

Z wrote back: *Me neither*

I wrote back: *Y?*

I held my breath until my phone vibrated again. The message read: *Couldn't stop thinking of u*

It took me a few minutes to stop trembling. I texted back: *Me neither*

I gazed out and saw Z looking at me from his house.

My phone vibrated: *Meet now?*

I wrote back: *Crutches*

His answer: *I'll come 2 u*

From my perch, I saw him disappear and then run out his front door and over to my yard. He vanished around the side of my house. It seemed like forever and then there he was hanging from a tree limb at the ledge tapping on my window.

I unlocked and pushed the pane open. He fell in and sat on the floor area in front of the window seat. I closed the window and sat beside him on the floor.

"We dress the same for bed," he remarked, noting our similar striped pajama bottoms and plain T-shirts. "Course I had to throw on shoes."

I glanced at his unlaced tennis shoes. "Shush, my sister's asleep really close." I motioned toward the other side of the room.

He smelled good. If I had any fear of him, it evaporated, as I was magically captivated.

"How'd you make it to the ledge?" I whispered.

"The tree house to the limb to here, not that hard." He spoke softly in his delightful voice.

"Our tree house?"

He nodded.

A few awkward moments of silence followed.

I scrunched up my face. "I don't usually do this. You know—

45

have strangers in my bedroom. As a matter of fact, I've never done this." I shook my head. "I don't even know why I am doing this." I wanted him to like me more than I had ever wanted anything in my whole life.

Z laughed quietly. "Me neither, but I knew I had to talk to you, to find out more about you. Weird, huh?"

"Bizarre. I've been having a lot of unusual things happen lately." For some inexplicable reason, I trusted him. Something about him made me feel safe.

"Me too." His smile dazzled. "It's a lot different here than in Alaska."

"I bet." I grinned back, trying to catch my breath. "Warmer, huh?"

We sat, not touching, for what seemed like a long time. I wanted to know about him. I *had* to know about him. "What's it like to live in Alaska?"

Sighing every once in a while as if in a dreamlike trance, I listened as he told about growing up in an Eskimo village in the upper reaches of Alaska. When Z talked, his eyes danced and sparkled. His voice lowered as he spoke of his mother home schooling all of the kids in the village. His chest widened boastfully as he shared that his father was a scientist studying the Aurora Borealis, the northern Alaskan lights. He told me anecdotes and personal stories until I felt totally immersed in his Alaskan life. Enthralled, I found everything he uttered fascinating. He was warm, open, and felt like home.

The clock from downstairs chimed midnight and I realized we'd been talking almost three hours.

His eyes softened. "What strange stuff's been happening to you?"

"If I tell you, you'll think I'm crazy." I studied him for reassurance. Didn't want to do anything wrong that would make him not like me. I wanted him to like me more than I'd ever wanted anything.

"I already think that." He offered and we chuckled.

I shushed him. "You really think I'm crazy?"

He locked eyes with me. "You invited a total stranger into your bedroom after I said hi."

"True." I had to admit he was right, but I couldn't explain to him why. How could I explain? I didn't even understand why I was doing these things.

"But I'm glad you did." He crossed his legs in a yoga-type position. "Ok, spill."

"I'm…" I stammered. "I'm having…" then I stopped and buried my head in my hands. " I don't think I can tell you."

"I told you my whole life story. A little reciprocation is warranted." He tried to peek under my hands.

"Big word." I scrunched my face and pursed my lips. "Want me to think you're smart?"

"Maybe I'm trying a little too hard for you to like me." He shifted uncomfortably on the floor.

"I *do* like you." Red heat rose through my neck and to my cheeks. I was so embarrassed I no longer cared if he thought I was crazy. "Okay, you asked for it. You might think I'm nuts, but I hear a voice and I think I might be able to read people's minds or that I am psychic or something. I got some books from the library to try to figure myself out."

Nervously, I pulled my backpack out from under my bed and pulled out the book about the test to see if you were psychic. I was afraid to lock eyes with him; I buried my head once again in my hands. "I know it sounds crazy."

I felt stupid. Of all of the idiotic things I had ever done in my life, this had to be the dumbest.

"I don't think you're crazy." He stroked my hair and I felt electrified. "I think you're the bravest person I've ever met."

I looked at him through watering eyes. "You do?"

He pulled my chin up with his hand and his touch exhilarated my being. "I think I know why I am drawn to you."

"Why?" I stammered, too enamored to get any other words out.

His eyes locked with mine. "All of that stuff has been

47

happening to me too."

Chapter 9

"Everything?" I asked, taken aback.

A light flashed on. "Leah?" Terra blasted through the beaded separator curtain.

With a loud thump, Z rolled under my bed.

"Yeah." I answered.

She jumped on my bed and peered over the side at me sitting on the floor. "What happened? Did you fall off the bed?"

"Yeah." I lied. I crawled onto my bed with her. "I musta had a dream or something and fell off."

"I thought I heard talking." She scooted off the bed and started back to her side of the room.

"I was probably talking in my sleep."

The beads of the separator curtain chimed as she retreated to her side of the room.

"Anyway thanks, for checking on me. G'night." I whispered out to her as I stretched out on my bed, not moving.

"Night." I heard a thump as she flopped on her bed. Terra's beside light went out.

I peered over the edge and threw Z one of the many extra pillows. He scooted out from under the bed and shoved the pillow under his head.

He whispered, "Do you think she'll go right back to sleep?"

"Probably." The moonlight illuminated his face. "You look like an angel."

"Not me. You. You're the one who has a face of an angel." He smiled and rubbed my arm. I trembled.

"Sorry." He mumbled and quickly moved his hand away.

"Don't be. Don't you feel it?" I moved my hand lightly over his bare arm.

"I do now." He rolled over and propped himself up on his side. "What is it with us? It's like we're..."

We both said at the same time. "...connected."

I said, "I didn't know if you felt it too." He dipped his head in agreement. I continued, "It's like we are magically in sync. Do you believe in reincarnation?" I asked.

"You mean like we were married or something in another life?" He touched my arm again, making me quiver.

"I dunno...could we have been family in another life?" I supported my head on my hand.

"Yuck. Like brother and sister." He pulled his hand away. "I don't have sisterly feelings for you."

I tingled inside. That's the first time in my whole life that a boy admitted he had feelings for me. I felt a rush of warmth. I wasn't sure what I was feeling, but I liked it and I didn't want it to end. I gazed into his moonlit face and memorized the curves of his chin and the golden specks in his eyes.

Our eyes locked for a few minutes more, and then he sat up. His face brushed against my arm. "I'd better go home. You need to get your rest. You were injured today."

I nodded. I was so full of emotion, I would have agreed to anything he said.

He crept out to the ledge and grabbed hold of the tree branch. "Can I come back another time?"

"Anytime." I stood at the window, thinking about him visiting again and sighed.

He gently brushed my hair out of my eyes. "Till next time." He leaped onto the limb and shimmied to the ground. I watched him run back across my yard and into his door. After a few minutes, he stood by his window as I stood by mine. He gave a little wave and disappeared. I fell on my bed. I had just met Z, but I felt as if I had known him all my life. I pulled the pillow that he had used and pressed it over my face. I inhaled his smell. Somehow, I had the feeling my life had just begun.

Not able to get back to sleep, I stared at the ceiling. I touched my forehead where Z had pushed the hair out of my eyes.

My cell buzzed announcing I had awaiting messages.

It was a text message from Kelly. Why was she writing this late? It must be important. I look at the time. No. She had written around ten, I hadn't check before now. What could it hurt to check what she had written?

She wrote: *Guess who likes u*

How could she know? It had just happened. What was she talking about? I had to find out who she was talking about.

I wrote back: *Who?*

A few minutes passed before she replied: *Heath Bolcan.*

It took me a moment to remember where I had heard that name. The boy who saved me from the truck. I had hardly looked at him.

Kelly texted again: *A rich senior likes u how cool is that?*

I knew it was late, but I also knew that Kelley was up so I called her. "Tell me exactly why you think this boy likes me."

"I saw Heath at the store this evening and he asked *do you know Leah Skye?* And I said yes."

I replied, "How did you get that he liked me from that?"

"Let me finish. He asked if we were going to the football jamboree game Friday night."

"What did you tell him?"

She answered, "I told him of course we'd be going since your brothers were on the team."

I sat silent for a few seconds. "So then what did he say?"

"He said that he would be going too since he played on the team and he'd like to meet up with us after the game."

51

I looked at the receiver. "That could mean that he likes you. Maybe he feels bad for me getting hurt and being on crutches. He could be using me to see you. Have you ever thought of that?"

Her voice whispered a muffled squeal. She was excited. "Do you think so? We are definitely going—if he's into me then we are definitely meeting up with him. You will come, won't you?"

"Of course."

My phone announced I had another call. It was Z. I had to end the call with Kelly. "I'll call you right back. Okay?" I didn't wait for an answer, I switched the call.

"Are you still awake? I can't sleep. I want to see you again. I need to see you again. Can I come over for a little while longer?" Z whispered into the phone.

"Yes." I trembled in anticipation. I was definitely breaking all the rules and I wasn't even fifteen yet. What was it about this boy?

I called Kelly back. I had to get the Heath problem taken care of. "Look it's late and we need to get some sleep, I think Heath likes you. See you tomorrow at school."

I ended the call quickly. I had to; Z was on his way over.

I walked into the bathroom, I brushed my hair and pinned one side back with a shiny clip. I sprayed some cinnamon body spray in the room and walked through it. I kissed at myself in the mirror as Terra came into the reflection.

Terra grabbed another clip from the bathroom counter and pinned her hair up. "I can't sleep. Who ya kissing—yourself?" She pranced in front of the mirror blowing kisses. "What's that smell?"

I shrugged and sprayed some cinnamon spray on her wrist. "It'll help you sleep."

She smelled her hand and mumbled, "*Um good.*"

Terra made her way through the beaded curtain. "Good night. See ya in the morning."

I grunted in her direction.

I texted Z: *sister awake. Wait a little*

I plopped on the bed. What a day! What a night! I was exhausted. My eyes labored to stay open. I closed my eyes for a moment and dreamed of Z.

My alarm buzzed loudly at six a.m. the next morning. Obviously, I had lost the battle to stay awake. A chocolate candy adorned my pillow along with a handwritten note. It read: *You are beautiful when you sleep. See you tomorrow at school.* He'd been here. He'd written a note. Who does that? My heart leapt. Z was different from any other boy.

I delicately folded the note and put it along with the candy in a small treasure chest made of cedar located on top of my dresser. Grabbing a quick breakfast, I hobbled out to the Camaro as Jorden climbed in the back seat.

Jorden tapped my crutches. "Guess I get the back seat now."

"Just for this week, then you're both in the back seat." Blue revved the engine as I situated myself in the front. Blue said, "We're giving my girl a ride to school."

Blue's girl was Kate Thomas. She was a senior with silky blonde hair that cascaded down to the middle of her back. A Florida girl: tan with flawless white teeth.

Ever since I had known her, she'd succeeded at everything. She'd been on the cheerleading squad at our old school. She excelled at athletics. She played volleyball in the fall and softball in the spring. Blue played two sports too, football and baseball. He was seventeen, almost eighteen and movie star handsome—everyone said so. They were the picture perfect couple—Barbie and Ken. Kate and Blue had been an item since as far back as I could remember. Sometimes, I thought they might have met in the crib.

We arrived at Kate's house, a ranch style one-story, half-brick, half-wood with a compact car parked in the drive. A basketball goal attached to the garage. A freestanding hammock and suspended swing along with azalea bushes and a large weeping willow tree decorated her yard. She ran out the door, stopped at Blue's window, and kissed him lightly on the lips.

"Leah's got the bum leg." He helped guide her in the backseat. "Seatbelt, Katie-girl."

She started talking the minute she hooked her belt. "Leah, this year I'm doing the dance squad instead of cheerleading. Wanted to try something new. Anyway, I signed you up for dance. I was helping with schedules Friday afternoon and I put you in my class for last period. It'll be loads of fun. They let me pick whoever I wanted. I put all the girls who had any dance experience. It'll be the best squad ever."

I didn't comment right away, so she continued. "I have a third cousin, Beth who's going to be on the squad and a girl from England, Constance and a couple of their friends. It'll be great."

Maybe I could talk her out of it. I'd have to try. I turned around and stared at this girl who had been such a fixture in our house she was part of the family. "Besides me having a bum ankle." I lifted a crutch. "I'm not much of a dancer." I hoped the girl from England wasn't our *friend* who insulted us daily.

"Give it a try." She batted her eyes and pursed her lips together in a pout. "For me," she finished in singsong fashion.

"Okay." No use in trying to get out of it. It could be fun and a way to meet other girls. Maybe if it was the same British girl, we could become friends. I knew whatever Kate wanted she got and as an added bonus, it would give me ammunition to hold over Blue. *Remember the time your girlfriend wanted me to be on the dance team and I didn't argue but did what she wanted—*

I was glad we had this conversation all the way to school. If we hadn't, all I would have been thinking about was Z.

Maybe I needed to see Z somewhere besides in the moonlight. Maybe he would be a little more human. Right now, I knew I had him so built up, he seemed perfect and flawless. No one could possibly be as wonderful as this person I had conjured up in my mind. Not even Z.

We pulled into the school parking lot. I glanced around the lot through my car window. There was Z—perfect and flawless. He was standing right there waiting on me alongside my two best friends, Kelly and Jane. How could I explain this?

Z trotted to my side of the car, grabbed my crutches from my lap, and pulled me out. Blue exited his side and helped Kate navigate out of the back seat. Jorden rolled his eyes at Blue fussing over Kate as he shifted out of the back seat. Then Jorden shot a confused glance Z's way.

Sensing the need for an explanation, I started. "This is Z, Stella's brother. You know Stella." About that time, Stella showed up. One thing about her was she did have great timing. "Here she is. Thanks for sending your brother to help me." Fortunately, she didn't seem to hear me or if she did, she didn't dispute me.

Everyone's confused and uncomfortable demeanor lightened. A little white lie never hurt anyone. Besides, how could I explain that Z had become a major part of my life because he spent a portion of *one night* in my room? Or I could confess we bonded because we could read minds and we heard voices? I chuckled. Ridiculous! Saying it out loud might mean a trip to the loony bin.

The British girl rushed up to Kate. "I'm so excited about dance class." And as she got out of earshot of Kate, she remarked to some of her friends, "Some people will do anything for attention— even feign an injury." I really disliked this girl and I guessed I was going to have dance class with her all year. Yuck!

I must have looked like Miss Popular Butterfly with my family, Z and Stella, Jane and Kelly helping me with my backpack and crutches.

I introduced them. "Z. This is Kelly and Jane, my best friends."

The bell reminded us it was time for school.

Z walked us to our building. "See ya at lunch." He winked secretly. I lit up without meaning to.

"Cute." Jane giggled as we separated to go to our respective homerooms.

Kelly crossed her fingers, disappearing down the hall. "Maybe we'll have some classes together."

Stella and I made our way to class, slowly on account of my crutches.

Clay waved as we came in. "What happened to you?" He seemed genuinely concerned; it made me feel awful that I had not counted him in my circle of friends and clued him in over the weekend. He had called me several times, but I never returned his calls.

I stumbled into my desk and decided a short answer would have to suffice for now. "Long story. Tell ya at lunch."

Mr. Grayson wasted no time passing out schedules. The three of us compared ours. We would have all the same academics, but different electives.

"Four out of six isn't bad." I reasoned with Kelly and Jane as we stood in the corridor after homeroom comparing our schedules. "We can do homework together sometimes."

The classes were set up so we had all of our academics in the morning, lunch, and then our two electives. That meant me, Jorden, Kelly, Jane, Clay, and Stella would travel together all morning.

The early morning academics dragged along as teachers seemed intent on going over the rules (again), introduction stuff, and passing out syllabi. The most thrilling thing that happened that morning was that I fell during one change between classes most certainly bruising my derrière.

Z texted me a couple of times during the class changes— humorous back and forth banter. I was anxious for lunch. I couldn't wait to see him. The powers that be had decided to stagger the lunches. That meant seniors got a head start by five minutes, juniors, the next five minutes, and us lowly sophomores brought up the rear.

Z was making his way to a table as we entered. "I got you some lunch today." He glanced at my group. "I thought it might be too hard to stand in line with your crutches." He shrugged.

"Thanks." I managed to get out before a freckle-nosed blonde girl crowded in behind Z. "Over here girls." She motioned and four others including the British girl came to the table. The blonde took a seat by Z. There was something about her. I couldn't put my finger on it but as drawn as I was to Z, I was equally repelled by this blonde intruder.

Z seemed surprised. "Oh, hey Bailey. Make sure to leave some seats. Leah has friends with her."

She furrowed her eyebrows. "Are you serious? Who is she,

your little sister or something?"

Z ignored the comment. "Bailey, this is Leah…Leah…Bailey. Bailey and I have physics together."

She snuggled in close to him. "We have a lot in common."

Z didn't pay attention to her again. I liked that. I didn't know her at all, but I already couldn't stand her.

A lot of scooting and shifting occurred as her group took their seats at our table. "Z this is Constance, she's from England." It was the British-accented girl—hated her. "And this is Beth, Iris, and Patra. Tell him how you got your name, Patra."

Patra, an olive-skinned girl, waved her hand. "It's not a big deal. I'm from Egypt, my mother named me Cleopatra—I use the end."

While the other girls tried their best to get his attention, Z whispered to me. "I've missed you." He slid my tray of food over and his hand brushed against mine ever so slightly, enough to send a tingle down my spine. "Not sure what you would eat, so I guessed."

Good guesses. I liked everything. "Here's my lunch money." I handed him a twenty. "Would you mind getting my lunch until," I pointed at my crutches, "I'm sprung from using these?"

"Trusting." He took the money out of my hand, lingering for a second, an electrical moment.

"Any reason I shouldn't be?" I took a bite of chicken sandwich trying not to lose myself in his eyes.

"Not at all." He deliberately grasped my hand. I quivered. When that would stop? I hoped never.

I wasn't as good as he was at pretending not to hear Constance and her posse. I cared what they said. I wanted him to like me. I didn't want those girls to ruin anything.

Constance's next remark hurt like a knife cutting into my heart. "Oh, some sort of a bet. Twenty bucks, huh? I knew there had to be something more. There had to be a reason why you hang out with *her*."

He ignored her as if he didn't even hear what she said. He was so intently concentrating on me that I don't think he did hear what she said. I had to admit I was enjoying watching her try to get his attention and him acting like I was the only one in the room, but it also got me to thinking. "My friends are going..." I whispered.

"Way ahead of you." He talked fast, but quietly. "Just act normal, after all we honestly did just meet today or rather yesterday, right?"

"Seems like I've known you forever." I looked down a little embarrassed. He released my hand as Kelly made her way to the table.

Introductions of everyone followed.

"Could you believe that get up Mr. Fitzsimmons was wearing?" Iris covered her mouth as she talked. "He came in full *Hamlet* costume complete with tights, velvet vest, feathered hat, the whole outfit."

 Everyone laughed.

Did Z feel the same exhilaration that I did when I was this close to him? I enjoyed sitting and talking with everyone and stealing glances with Z as if we were in on some kind of a private joke. Was he now my boyfriend?

Jane and Clay liked each other right away. I knew Jane well enough to see it. They were alike in many ways. When Heath joined us, Kelly zeroed in on him. Kelly always went after whatever she wanted. She was definitely not shy. Since Z had ignored Constance's advances, she moved on to Heath. If I were a betting person, my money would be on Kelly. Stella and my brother, Jorden, looked like they kind of liked each other. Was this going to be the year that everyone in Berry paired off?

Lunch was over way too early. As the bell rang, I exchanged a secret glance with Z and he touched my hand lightly as I hobbled off to the weight room. My mood was so cheerful that I even had high hopes for weightlifting—like maybe it would get me in shape.

I arrived a few minutes late for class.

Heath Bolcan met me at the door. "I've signed us up for partners. I hope you don't mind."

Chapter 10

"I don't mind. Thanks for signing me in. I've been late to about every class." I struggled to sit on a weight bench and glanced around. Everyone did seem to have partners.

"I never got a chance to thank you for saving me from the truck. Thanks."

He smiled. "No problem."

"You're huge." I stared at Heath and added, "No offense, but how am I supposed to spot you?"

"No offense taken. I *know* I'm huge." He flexed his muscles. "Don't worry. They don't trust any of us. They have all kinds of volunteers to do the actual spotting."

Adult spotters were strategically placed around a room filled with weight benches, lifting machines, elliptical units, treadmills, bicycles, mats, and bar weights. Large water bottle dispensers and sports drink machines were intermixed with the exercise equipment. Huge bins for towels labeled *used* and *fresh* sat in front of a wall display decorated with various checklists and charts.

"Okay. Works for me." I noticed everyone was wearing shorts and T-shirts. "I really don't want to dress out."

He sat down on the weight bench beside me. "I told them you were on crutches. The teacher excused you." He pointed to the far end of the room. "There are boys' and girls' locker room complete with locked personal storage units." He held up his wrist, showing a slinky type bracelet holding a key. "You wear the key while you exercise."

"Nice. Nothing but the best, although I'm surprised our

barcodes aren't on those keys." I grinned.

"Maybe they are." He chuckled.

I rubbed my knee. "I think I'm going to like this school and all of the people. Everyone's been helping me all day."

"You really don't know why everyone is helping you? Do you?" As he lifted a weight over his head, two spotters hurried to assist him. He had muscular arms—really defined.

"Duh, crutches?" I held out a crutch.

He placed the weight in its holster, sat up, and playfully tapped me on the forehead. "Duh? No, it's because you're the prettiest girl in school." He waved the spotters away. "I'm taking a break for a minute." They moved back.

I shifted my weight uncomfortably on the bench. "What?" I caught a glimpse of myself in the mirrored covered walls in the weight room. I didn't see it. I looked the same. I'd never been thought of as pretty. I've always been a bit chunky, but I *had* lost some weight over the summer. My clothes were so big I had to get a new wardrobe while in Washington. But pretty? Kate was gorgeous. Kelly and Jane were pretty. Patra, an exotic beauty. Yes, even though I hated to admit it, Constance was strikingly lovely. Me, not so much.

I shrugged. "Do you need glasses?"

He motioned the spotter back and lifted the weight. "Guys have thought it. They might not have said it, and no, I don't need glasses. Why do you think I grabbed you out of the road? I noticed you in the library. I thought you were pretty. I was hoping to meet you and you—"

"Fell in a hole," I finished his sentence. He almost dropped the weight bar laughing with me, causing the spotters to gasp.

He did a few more reps. "I think I'll move to this machine. Don't need spotters for this. Thanks." The spotters left as I flipped my feet over the bench and twirled around.

He changed the weight amount, and then pulled down the bar. Sweat dripped down his biceps. "I asked your friend Kelly if you were going to the game Friday night."

Ut-oh. "Yeah, she told me." I didn't like where this

conversation was going so I blurted out, "Kelly likes you. She wants to meet up with you after the football game."

He loosened his grip and the weight clanged. "W…w…well," he stuttered. It was the first time he didn't seem sure of himself. "I actually wanted to meet up with *you*."

I liked him, but I was already with Z. I didn't really want to tell anyone about that yet so I lied, or at least I didn't tell the whole truth.

"Oh gosh. I hadn't really thought of you that way. When Kelly told me about you, she had gotten the impression that you were interested in her. Did you know Kelly is one of my very best friends? I'm sorry, but she's such a close friend…" I stopped, held my breath, and waited.

He took the hint. "Okay. I get it."

"You're going to love Kelly. She's perfect. You know her family has a lake house, she enjoys movies, and she'll love watching you play football. Honestly, she would get a kick out of being your partner in this weightlifting class."

He stared at me as I babbled on and then began his reps again. He finally stopped my chattering by saying, "Okay, okay, Kelly it is. I'll see you *and* Kelly Friday night after the game."

"Sure." Relief flooded over me.

I found out a lot about Heath as he went through his routine. He'd grown up on the Big Island of Hawaii—lived there his whole life. He attended private school and resided on a large pineapple plantation that his family had owned for generations. Florida weather reminded him of home.

As we talked, I realized he was kind of a sweetheart. I knew Kelly would like him. What was not to like? He was gorgeous and in one of those ways where you think somebody is nice looking and then the more you get to know them the prettier or more handsome they get. I had to admit from the time the weightlifting class had started until now; Heath had gotten a lot better looking. Must be that inner beauty my mother was always clamoring about.

I was actually sad when the bell rang for the next class, but I couldn't wait to text Kelly about Heath. She called me immediately.

She screamed loud in the phone. "I can't believe it. I'm going out with a senior!" She squealed again. "What should I wear?"

"We'll talk later. I'm already late for class." I ended the call and headed for dance.

"Finding your way without my help?" It was the boy from the first day.

Still sporting the high from Kelly's enthusiasm, I was all full of myself and brave. "My name's Leah. I don't think you ever told me your name. I'll call you, let me see—*Guide*. Okay, Guide, where's the gym?"

"Name's Stone." He pointed down the hall. "The gym is this way. I'm headed there. I'll walk with you."

I hobbled along trying to keep up and failing miserably.

He gained a few steps, turned around, and asked, "What class do you have next?"

I shouted to him, "I've got dance. What about you?"

He doubled back and headed toward me. "I'm Coach's student assistant this period." He startled me as he grabbed my crutches, handed them to me, and picked me up in his arms. "I'll carry you. Seems you're struggling, and I can't be late. I have to take roll."

The doors were open to the classes. As we walked by one, I saw Kelly and Z sitting in desks watching me. Z looked none too happy. I locked eyes with him and tried to give him a quick—*this-was-not-my-idea*—expression. Stone carried me so fast I didn't have time to see if I had conveyed the meaning.

At the gym, I wasn't able to participate or to use my phone, as we had to deposit our book bags on the bleachers. Stone helped me drop mine off and plopped me down on the gym floor with the others in the dance class before heading off.

The hairs on the back of my neck bristled. I wondered why, and then I scanned the room. Yep, there they sat, Constance and her friends.

Kate wrinkled her brow. "So getting carried to class by a seriously cute upperclassman. You aren't having such a bad day, are you?"

Constance lifted her eyebrows and put her hands on her hips as she sat cross-legged on the floor. "You need to make up your mind. I thought you were flirting with that other guy at lunch." Then she mouthed where only I could see, "Tramp."

Kate looked over at me, confused. "What boy?'

I didn't know what to say. Luckily, the choreographer interrupted, spouting out her vision for our dance class. At least I didn't have to try to finagle my way out of that question, but there was still the matter of Z. I didn't want him to get the wrong impression. Time dragged on. Constance asked so many questions of the dance instructor, I thought I was going to vomit.

I hoped I'd have a chance to see Z before the bus, to explain what was going on. I wanted him to like me more than anything I'd ever wanted. I couldn't imagine him thinking about me as much as I thought about him.

I didn't have to wonder long. Z found me before I picked up my backpack from the bleachers.

"Are you all right? I saw you being carried, and then you didn't answer your cell." He touched my arm. "You scared me. I can carry you to the car if you need me to." What a dreamboat. How gallant was that?

"No, I'm fine. We couldn't take our cells to class. I can hobble. Besides, I ride the bus home." I leaned over to pick up my stuff.

He grabbed my backpack. "Do you ride all the way? Don't you have to walk some?" I nodded and he continued, "I don't think you should walk home on that ankle."

I rubbed my ankle. It *was* swollen up—more than this morning. He was probably right.

I said, "I guess I could call Mom and see if she could pick me up after Terra."

"Good idea. You can watch football practice till she comes." He helped me sit on an outside bench while I called.

Mom agreed and said she was sorry she hadn't thought of it.

Z headed for practice after I refused to let him carry me. He took my stuff so I could maneuver more easily. I limped with the crutches, taking my time, and finally sat on the grass next to where Z had placed my backpack. A chocolate candy sat on top of the pack. Z sure was sweet—as sweet as that candy. I ate it since I wouldn't be able to save this one. There's nothing better than half-melted chocolate filling your mouth. I made it last as long as I could, swishing it around savoring every last morsel. Delicious!

Constance, along with her group—Bailey, Iris, Patra and Beth—pretended to practice a dance routine, but all they wanted was the football team's attention. It worked. They were such a distraction that the coach made the girls move.

I watched as my brothers, Z, and Heath ran a variety of plays. Jorden didn't miss anything and Z seemed to read every play. He even sacked Blue a few times. Heath played both the offensive and defensive lines. Heath was about the only player who could stop Z. I wondered if the Berry Bears would be a good team.

Starting back to school all day had been exhausting and staggering around on the crutches had made it much harder.

That evening, I pulled out a *West Side Story* assignment for English from my backpack.

My phone vibrated. A text from Z. *Set phone 4 2am*

I texted back: *Gr8 idea*

For the first time in my life, I had a boyfriend even if I couldn't say it out loud.

At two that morning, I rolled over and turned off my vibrating phone. Z rested on my floor looking up at me with those dreamy eyes. I'd left the window open so he could get in. I'd always been the good girl obeying all the rules. Now I was in the dark with a boy and keeping the whole thing a secret. No, not at all like me—I might have been concerned except all decisions that excluded seeing Z went right out when he was near. I studied his eyes, the almond-shaped windows into his soul—unusual coloring—black around the edges and lighter brown turning almost amber toward the middle. I had no idea what color to call his eyes so I would describe them as Z-colored eyes. I was hexed. Bottom line—I had to see him—no, more than that, I lived to see him. How is that possible? I'd only met him a day ago.

"Hey, sleepy head." He brushed my hair as it draped over the side of the bed. "I missed you today."

"Missed you too." I dropped my arm and he pulled me effortlessly on the floor beside him, careful not to jar my ankle. I could stay right here forever.

I froze, listening for Terra. Hearing no movement, I pulled two pillows off my bed.

"I want to try something." I whispered in his ear. Being this close to him made me dizzy.

He rolled over and propped up on his arm. "What?"

I rolled closer and slung my arms around him.

He blocked me. "Whoa! What'd you want to try?"

"Sorry." I shrank back. "You're going to think this is crazy."

He shifted. "What?"

I supported myself on my arm and faced him. "I want to try and see if we can read each other's minds."

He smiled. "Interesting."

"What does *The Voice* sound like to you?" I asked.

He dropped back down, pensive. "A voice that I recognize, but not really, kinda garbled."

I whispered. "I don't recognize *The Voice*. What does yours say?"

He propped back up. "Different things. Haven't heard it in a while."

My eyes got big. "I haven't heard it either. Why do you think we haven't?"

He rubbed his temple. "It could be because *The Voice* was only for us both to hear and to bring us together and now that it has—the job is done."

"What a romantic thought." I leaned over close to him again and once again, he backed up.

He touched my hair. "Let's do what you wanted to do—try to read my mind."

65

Chapter 11

"**B**ut before we start—" He held my chin in his hand. "I was raised in Alaska with a remote Eskimo tribe. We're different."

I scrunched my face and pursed my lips. "How?"

"We don't get physical until—" He stopped.

I wanted to know what he meant. "What kind of physical—kissing, hugging, touching, what?"

He tightened his grip on my chin. "I grew up believing we mate for life. Do you understand?"

"So no kissing." I lifted my eyebrows. "No hugging?"

"Has your mother ever had the grown-up talk with you?" He leaned on his hand and made his face wrinkle.

I touched his hand. "I know stuff." I couldn't hide my embarrassment.

He let go of my chin and propped his head up. "You've never had a boyfriend?"

I frowned. "No, I haven't really been interested in boys till now."

"How old are you?"

"Almost fifteen. How old are you?"

"I'm sixteen, but I've been told I have an old soul. Growing up as I did, I sort of skipped childhood. We grow up faster. We have to."

He smiled sweetly. "Your mother might have a talk with you when she finds out you're seeing somebody." He stared intently in my eyes and I was lost in his.

Quiet took over which made me uncomfortable, so I said the

first thing that popped into my head. "Okay, can we try the mind reading thing now?"

He chuckled. I recited the steps to read someone's mind and he played along. We sat with our hands on each other's heads, blanked our minds, and concentrated. Z. Nothing. I focused harder. Z. Nothing. I took all thoughts out of my mind. Nothingness took over.

I woke up to my alarm. I must have fallen asleep and Z must have placed me in my bed before leaving. Figured one thing out though, I couldn't read his mind.

I don't know if it was meeting Z, but now food tasted more delicious. Everything smelled better. Life seemed to be a little sweeter. My senses exploded. I had found that little kid's remote gizmo in the bushes that he couldn't see. I could hear and see things better than others could see or hear. Z mentioned he'd noticed the same things.

I looked forward to Friday when I would be free of the crutches. I loved going to school because every day Z would meet me at the car.

Classes were enjoyable or at least I enjoyed them. Maybe everything seemed better because of Z. I didn't know. We wrote a lot and broke into study groups. In English class, we read parts in *West Side Story*. My bunch always grouped together which made it even better.

In honors biology, we were going to dissect things and study cadavers. This was especially important, since I planned to be a doctor when I grew up. Funny all of the sudden, I started feeling more grown up.

The high school clique was in full force. Clay and Jane found a group of students who were interested in discussing solutions for the woes of the world, books they had read, and projects they were working on.

The football players crowded together to discuss plays from the night before or games that would be played soon. Constance and her clique found excuses to pal up with this group. It wasn't hard to imagine why.

The artsy crowd spent time sharing their poetry, paintings, or sculptures. Writers would read their original stories or share graphic drawings.

There were factions of people who knew each other from their old schools. Other places and cultures were represented: Z from Alaska, Heath from Hawaii, Patra from Egypt, Constance from England, Iris from Russia, and Beth from Israel. It was a melting pot of cultural diversity.

I worked hard on the dance routines, hobbling best I could through them because the Dance Team was performing at the half time show for the Jamboree and for the pep rally. My bandage would be off by Friday, but it would take at least a week to get the ankle working again. Constance volunteered and reveled in taking my place.

Every afternoon I watched the boys practice, went home, finished my homework took a nap, ate, got ready for bed and waited for my favorite part of the night: Z's visits. We tried the "How to tell if you are a Psychic" test. We both failed miserably. We looked into hormones and causes for heightened senses. Nothing we found explained it. It was weird. Whatever was happening was happening to both of us. We even searched pheromones, a sort of animal magnetism that drew people together. We agreed we had some sort of magnetism, whether it was pheromones or not.

All of this "voice and sense" business should have upset us, but it brought us closer together. Having someone to talk to about stuff made things seem a little less scary. I couldn't remember my life before Z. The only thing that terrified me now was life without Z.

I sat down with Z at lunch on Friday. "What're you doing this afternoon?"

"Nothing after the pep rally." He pushed my lunch tray over to me. "I have to be here for the game tonight, but we have about three hours after school before that. Want me to come over?"

"I was planning to ride home with Blue. What about me coming over to your house?" I tried to read his face for the answer. He lit up, a good sign.

He bit into his fish sandwich. "Better yet, let's ride the bus home together. Then you come over."

I ate a French fry. "I like that plan. My ankle is better and I can walk on it today."

The others joined us at the lunch table, including Constance and her friends, after they stopped to talk to some football players.

Jorden squeezed in by Stella and glanced at me. "You gonna ride home with us today?"

I peeked at Z. "No I thought I'd take the bus if that's okay." Then added, "I need to exercise the ankle. It might atrophy."

The group laughed.

Jorden commented, "Big word, sis." He shoved his shoulder playfully into Stella. "Why don't you take her place, Stella, and ride home with us?"

Stella looked at me. "I don't want to desert Leah."

Clay smiled. "Don't worry, I'll be there."

Bless you Clay— you came through when I needed you.

Kelly took a fry off Heath's plate. "What's everyone doing after the game?"

"Going to Pearl's," Jane said matter-of-factly.

Everyone in town knew about Pearl's, a local diner. It had a sports-type bar area over to the side, the owner used it during college and pro sports game nights to sell wings and beer. On high school game nights, he opened it up to the local high school and sold burgers, fries, and soft drinks.

"Then a spend-the-night at the lake house," Kelly added. "My mom will pick us up at Pearl's. Bring your stuff to the game."

There was no getting out of that. Kelly, Jane, and I had done that every Friday night for as long as I could remember. If the weather allowed, we'd go to the lake house.

I glanced at Z. "Why don't you come to the lake on Saturday? We could show you where Kelly's house is. You'd have a good time. We could go canoeing or swimming."

Z smiled. "Sure. I love the lake. My family stayed there before we officially moved in our house."

The announcement boomed out over the loud speaker. "Please excuse the dance team, cheerleaders, football players, and band to go to the field to set up for the pep rally."

Catching up with Kate, I laughed. "That should cover the whole school."

I giggled again and then remembered Jane and Kelly. I quit laughing and thought, *Quit being so full of yourself—you have a boyfriend on the football team and are on the dance squad and now you think you are all that.* I hated that kind of thinking even if it was me thinking that way.

I walked into the gym and took my place with the dancers. I was introduced as a member of the Bear Hugs Dance Squad. Constance pranced out when her name was called. She was such a show off. I despised her.

Everyone cheered each football player's name as he was introduced. I screamed especially loud for Z and my brothers, and got a good ovation when I was introduced. "Good" meaning I wasn't embarrassed by a lack of cheering.

The cheerleaders led everyone in a chant about stomping the opposing team and the dancers, except me, strutted their stuff. Constance over-emphasized her dance moves, yet another effort to have all eyes on her.

The best part of the pep rally was that we got out about ten minutes early, and ten minutes more with Z was priceless.

Z found me immediately afterwards. "Hey, beautiful."

"Hey, yourself." I pushed my shoulder into his and felt the electrical connection.

His face glowed. Wow, he was gorgeous.

What a great afternoon! I was excited about finally seeing Z's room.

I laughed as we walked to the bus. "You know if we end up together, you will literally be the boy next door."

Z corrected. "The boy across the street. And what do you mean *if?*"

I squeezed into my familiar spot beside Clay for the ride home. Z took Stella's place by L.H.

Clay talked incessantly all the way to our bus stop about the pep rally. Seemed like forever before Z and I finally reached our destination.

"I'm kinda excited to see your room." I limped cautiously on my ankle.

"Hope you're not *too* disappointed." He pushed his shoulder playfully into mine, almost causing me to lose my balance.

"Nothing about you would ever disappoint me." I grabbed his wrist to steady myself. "If it's yours, then it's perfect."

He held my palm softly and we walked down the street hand in hand.

I pulled out my cell with my free hand. "I'm going to call my mom and leave her a message so she won't worry."

We arrived at his house and all was quiet. He tried the door, but it was locked. He pulled out his key, unlocked the door, and inched it open. "Anybody home?" He paused a minute. "Apparently not. Maybe Stella's over at your house." We both laughed a bit and entered.

You could tell that they still had a little unpacking to do. The house was full of big ornate pieces that looked decades old.

"I like your house." I stood in his foyer.

Z shut the door. "Glad you do. Want something to drink?" He led me into the kitchen—warm, cozy, and very yellow.

"Sure." I picked up a sun motif trivet. "Your mom likes yellow, huh?"

"It was this color when we moved in, but yes, she likes sun and star decorations, and so does my dad." He pulled two cans of grape soda out of the refrigerator. "Follow me."

We walked up the stairs and he pointed out his Mom and Dad's room, Neb's, and Stella's room.

He swung the door open. "And this is the Z room. Hope you're not too disappointed."

He made his way to the window. "This is where I saw you for the very first time." I stood by him.

He smiled. "Right from this spot."

We watched as Mom and Terra arrived. I said, "There's Mom."

He sat back on his bed and patted it. I sat down beside him.

I picked up a picture album off his bedside and opened it. There were pictures of a smiling adorable toddler by an enormous snowman. Another showed a small boy in the seat of a plane in a field of snow. "Are these you?"

"Yes." We scooted down on our stomachs on his bed. He spent a few minutes flipping through the album, identifying his extended family, grandmother, grandfather, and the people in the village where he grew up. He went into detail about the supply plane that came every six months when he came to the picture of him sitting in its cockpit. Not sure how long we had been looking through the album. I always lost track of time when I was with Z. A loud sound startled me.

Z rolled on his back. "Is that your phone?"

I retrieved my cell from my pocket. "Probably my mom."

I answered. "Hey Mom...yes I'm across the street...me and ..." I stopped for a minute. I knew honesty would be the only way to go. "...and Z...he's Stella's brother...yeah...we can come across the street...yeah" I shrugged. "...yeah, he wanted to meet you too...We'll be over in a minute."

"You gotta go meet my mom. Stella's there. She told my mom I was here. We gotta go public sometime."

He held both my hands in his and rubbed them softly. "Then it's official. We're going together."

I squeezed his hands. "Do I get a ring?"

"One day." He whispered in my ear and my heart jumped a beat. "Leah, you're probably gonna hear that grown-up talk this afternoon."

Chapter 12

We walked over to my house and I introduced Z. He couldn't stay long as he had to get back for football.

After he left, Mom came into my room. "We need to have a little talk."

I love my mom, but sometimes I wished she wasn't so predictable. I liked having secrets. Z was only mine and I liked it that way. My mom asked too many questions. I didn't want her getting so much in my business.

I wasn't completely clueless. I knew about kissing and hugging and all that. I'd had the talk about my period. My mom was a nurse so she went through a very sweet explanation about what she thought love was and a talk about being smart and not having babies without wanting them.

"Mom, we haven't even kissed."

She jerked so quickly her charm bracelet jangled—each of the charms was a heart locket with a baby picture of one of us on one side and a current picture on the other side; five hearts, one for each of us and one for my dad and her. "It's not that I don't want you to have a boyfriend. I want you to be prepared. Now about birth control—"

"Grace! I told you we haven't even kissed." I shouted and then calmly added. "But if things start going that way I'll come and talk with you I promise." I grabbed her hand and squeezed it. "Gah, Mom. Sometimes I wish you'd make things easy. I *promise* to come and ask you about it."

"I believe you will." She turned back to me and poked my

forehead with her index finger. "Be smart."

She didn't know that Z was the one being smart. Mom used the word *intimate* over and over. I knew from my vocabulary words in English classes that intimate meant "closely personal and warmly cozy." I guess if my mom didn't want me to get intimate with Z, it was too late. Those two descriptions illustrated our relationship exactly. I repeated in my head *closely personal and warmly cozy*. I beamed. Yes, that described me and Z. The physical stuff would have to wait. We didn't need it, at least not now.

"Here come the fighting Berry Bears!" The announcer's voice boomed in the stadium. Our dance team marched on the field with our band at the beginning of the game along with all bands from other high schools and played *The Star Spangled Banner* as everyone sang. It was the only time during the year that all of the teams would be together. That's what jamborees were all about. The stands were filled to capacity. I sat with our band during our part of the game. I was on the field during half time for the performance. It was exhilarating listening to the crowd cheer. I especially enjoyed it when Z waved at me as he ran onto the field.

Constance back-flipped a few times on the field after she dominated the dance routine. "Such a show off." I liked her even less now. It was amazing how tolerant Kate was, but how could Kate be bothered by anyone, she had no competition—Kate with her perfect self.

The Bears controlled the first quarter easily, struggled in the third, but ultimately won. I was glad because everyone would be happy. Plus, the Bears *were* my team and I wanted them to win.

"Go Bears!" Kelly and Jane shouted as I ran up to them after the game.

"Girls—this way." Mom and Dad motioned to our car.

At Pearl's, Dad asked, "Kelly's mom is picking you girls up, right?"

Kelly grabbed my overnight case. "Yes, Mr. Skye. She should be here in a couple of hours." She looked at Jane and me. "Jane, bring your case. We can store them in the back of Pearl's."

Kelly scored a table up front. "Glad we beat most of the people here."

We ordered, sat, and waited for the football players to arrive.

Blue came in first and the place cheered. "Where's my Kate?" Kate gave him a big hug and murmured something in his ear. They took off to a secluded table in the back.

"Mind if I sit here?" Z surprised me by sneaking in before I saw him. Kelly scooted over to the next seat making room for him. I figured by now that everyone knew we were a couple.

Heath sat with Kelly. "Can Brett join us?"

Kelly nodded. Could Heath have a plan that involved Kelly liking the other guy better? Didn't really care as long as Kelly was happy.

Astrid, Heath's sister, seemed to be hitting it off with Neb, Z's older brother. Heath's family had a Hawaiian look, maybe from their mother.

I laughed. Everyone is pairing off. Who would be together at the end of the year? That was anybody's guess.

Constance, along with Patra, Iris, and Beth flirted up with some other football players. Did Constance wear that wide leather bracelet all the time? Always had it on. It had a design, but I had not figured it out yet. I'd ask her if we ever talked. Maybe I would never find out, I chuckled to myself.

Kelly's mom walked in. The room got quiet. "Time to go."

Z leaned close and whispered in my ear. "I'll miss you in the middle of the night."

I took his hand lightly and murmured, "Me too. But I'll see you tomorrow. Right?"

"Definitely." He stood and pulled my chair out for me.

True to form, we girls slept in. It was after 11 A.M. before we took showers, changed into bathing suits, and made our way to Central Lake. Most of the gang was already there, including Z.

75

Kelly pointed to the lake. "Hey look—there's that crazy boat driver again." The boat drove right next to where we were sitting and Neb, Z's brother, got out. My mouth dropped open.

Kelly angrily yelled. "You know you almost killed my friend."

Neb helped Astrid out. "What are you talking about? What friend?"

"Your boat, a couple of weeks ago." Kelly said.

Neb rubbed his hand across the motor on the back. "This boat—just rented it. This is the first time I've driven it."

I grabbed Kelly and slowly whispered, "Never mind. Please don't make a thing of this—drop it." I remembered the star tattoo and surveyed Neb's arm—no tattoo. Same boat—different driver.

Fortunately, Heath walked in. "Hey." He sat down beside me.

Z made his way over and sat with us. "I heard you're helping my girl with her weightlifting."

Heath cocked his head. "Yeah. That's not a problem, is it?" Heath and Z locked eyes.

I jumped in. "Of course not, you're the best partner a girl could have."

Z finished. "*My girl* deserves the best."

From then on, everyone knew I was Z's girl. When Z walked up, people would move to give him the seat beside me. If I hadn't noticed Z was around, people would point him out. We were definitely connected and everyone knew it; even Kelly and Jane who had been my best friends forever, backed away. My family asked about him daily like he was a part of the family. It was magical—like it was meant to be. I was happier than I'd ever been in my whole life.

The next two months were idyllic. I would go to school and see Z. He secretly visited me most nights. Mom's bracelet jangling warned of her approach and Terra slept like a dead person so it was easy to talk undisturbed. The family was worried about my afternoon naps, but how could I function on no sleep. I had to get it sometime. Z took naps too. Even though, we had altered our sleep patterns, we were still able to get everything done. School, after-school activities, friends, everything. I loved my life right now and never wanted it to change.

We wrote silly little poems to each other. I kept them all in the treasure box on my dresser, along with the first note and the chocolate candy that had accompanied it.

My happiness grew. Neither he nor I had heard *The Voice*. We forgot about wondering if we could read minds or if we were psychic. If he wasn't over at my house for dinner or to visit, I was over at his. We'd go to the lake, out to eat, to the mall, or to watch a movie, but always together. Z became part of my life; I couldn't imagine a time without him. He was an extension of who I was—he was a part of me and when he wasn't around a piece of me was missing.

I was getting better at dance thanks to Kate and was getting stronger thanks to Heath. Even Constance didn't grate as much on my nerves.

Mine and Jorden's birthday was fast approaching. We decided to have a party at the Lake recreational center.

The night before my birthday, Z came over to my house at 2 A.M., our usual time.

"I got you a present." He handed me a box. "I didn't wrap it. Sorry."

"That's okay." I took the top off and pulled out a piece of jewelry.

"It's an anklet." He beamed, grabbed it out of my hand, and pulled my foot up to him. "I'll put it on you. I thought it was appropriate since you had a hurt ankle the first time I saw you."

I smiled. "So I did."

"It has hearts all around it." He clicked it on my ankle.

"I'll wear it always." I touched his cheek. He touched mine. We sat there for a long time gazing into each other's eyes. I breathed him in. I wondered how my feelings could possibly grow any more, but every day they did.

"I better go. You've got a big day planned." He leaned over and touched his lips to my cheek lightly. "See you tomorrow."

It was the most romantic thing that had ever happened to me. A perfect kiss on the cheek and a perfect present from a perfect boyfriend. I couldn't wait for the rest of my life.

Exhilaration followed me to school the next day, as everyone wished me a happy birthday. I showed off my anklet and embarrassed Z. Lots of students planned to attend our birthday party on Saturday, two days away. The football team was playing Friday and had been doing really well—only one loss to a big school from down south.

We had our family dinner and celebration the night of our birthdays. Z, Stella, Kelly, and Jane came over before, but left so our family could have our time together. My parents liked the anklet. Of course, I lied and told them he had given it to me at school. My parents gave me a new cell, which I needed, and some money. Jorden received the same thing. Terra made me a decoration for my dresser.

Kelly got me a sun catcher. "I loved mine so much, thought you might like one too." She was right. It was a star and sparkled when the light hit it.

Jane gave me a CD she had made of all of our favorite music. "I knew you had to have some of Justin. I even added his new song."

Mom came into my room right before I went to sleep that night. "Hope you've had a good birthday so far. There's one more thing that we want you to have, Leah." She handed and old box to me. It was tattered and worn. The hinges almost fell apart as it creaked open. Inside was a necklace with a red stone beautifully encased in gold with one diamond attached at the top.

"This was your grandmother's. It has been passed down generation to generation." Mom carefully took it out of the box and put it around my neck.

"A ruby, right?" I asked.

She nodded and I continued, "I've never *seen* such a beautiful ruby." I walked over to the mirror. The red stone sparkled.

"And you won't. It was mined by your ancestors from the ruby mines of North Carolina." She smiled at me with tears in her eyes. "She would have wanted you to have it. I'm sorry she's not here to share this moment."

"Me too. Thanks, Mom." I threw my arms around her neck.

Memories of my grandmother flooded my mind. My grandparents' early demise prompted Mom to escape with Terra and me for the summer. She needed the break from the sorrow. I know she missed them, I sure did.

Z had told me earlier he wouldn't be coming over. I would have to wait to show him the necklace tomorrow.

That night I had a dream where someone said, "You possess the bloodstone." I woke up afraid, but the thought of Z calmed me enough to fall back asleep.

The next morning, I felt my new jewelry. The anklet and the necklace. I stared at myself in the mirror with the necklace. How it sparkled! I went downstairs and glanced at one of the pictures of my grandmother on the mantel. She wore the ruby.

"Mom, why didn't you ever wear the necklace?" I grabbed a breakfast bar.

Mom glanced up. "I did when I was younger. Got it when I got married. I actually had to put it away when I had you. You kept pulling at it. You broke it once and I had it fixed." She took the necklace in her hand and stared at it. "It's a lovely piece. Maybe you only wanted it for yourself." She chuckled.

I smiled. "Maybe so."

I was anxious to get to school that day. I was fifteen. I felt so grown up. I had a boyfriend and an anklet to prove it.

Z wasn't waiting for me at the parking area like he usually did. I texted and tried to call him. No answer. I didn't worry, I'd see him at lunch. The school was abuzz about our joint birthday party. Talk about it kept my mind occupied and I was glad for the distraction.

Lunch came and no Z. I began to worry when I connected that Stella was also absent from all of the morning classes.

Jorden came to lunch and I asked him, "What's going on with Z and Stella?"

Jorden inspected his phone. "Not sure. Haven't seen her since yesterday. She didn't answer my text or call. I'll try again."

After school, I ran from the bus stop. Maybe he was sick or something happened with his family. Why didn't he call and explain? It was strange. When I got to his house, it was locked. No car in the driveway. The morning paper was still out in the yard and the mail hadn't been picked up. I went around the back. I peeked in his window. No sign of anyone.

I went to my house and sat on the porch swing to wait for Mom. When she came, I told her. "Mom, Stella or Z didn't come to school. I'm worried."

"Did you try to call?" She asked matter-of-factly.

I raised my voice. "Grace, don't you think I would have tried that first?"

Mom sat down beside me and brushed my hair with her hand. "Look, I'm sure everything is fine."

I fumed. Why couldn't she understand how upsetting this was for me? I was so mad with her I couldn't see straight. I went to my room to get ready for the game. I calmed myself down. Z wouldn't miss the game.

At the football game, I went through the motions of the dance, but my heart wasn't in it. I kept looking on the field, but no Z—no Neb—no Stella.

Constance danced by. "Where's your boyfriend?"

I hated her.

My birthday party was the next day. Z wouldn't miss that. I would find out soon what was going on and then we would have a big laugh about how upset I'd been. I went home right after the game and helped Mom, Kelly, and Jane with the party preparations, trying to keep my mind off Z, but it didn't work. I kept looking across the street all night. No sign of anyone coming home. What happened to them?

Party night came.

No Z.

No Stella.

No word.

No explanation.

No nothing.

Jorden and I were depressed. We tried to keep up appearances, but it was hard. I must have left a jillion messages. I was desperate. It was like they had vanished off the face of the earth. Where was Z? I felt empty inside. I tried again to reach out to him, to *think* him to me. We were connected from a psychic point of view or whatever it was. I knew we were.

After my party, I told Kelly I felt sick and had to go home. She didn't believe me. She knew what was wrong. When I got home, I fell into bed. I sobbed uncontrollably in my pillow for a while and then tried to speak to Z telepathically. It was a crazy thing to do, but I was desperate.

I focused with all my might. *The Voice* had to talk to me. I needed it.

I screamed in my mind. *"TELL ME WHERE Z IS!"*

Chapter 13

I sat up in my bed. Nothing

I repeated in my head. *Where's Z?*

No success.

I beat my fists on the bed, kicked my legs, and had a good old-fashioned temper tantrum. I needed Z. I was lost without him.

Exhausted, I finally sprawled on the bed and fiddled with the ruby necklace. I took the necklace off and placed it on the dresser.

My phone vibrated. I answered.

IT WAS Z.

"I can't talk long. We had a death in the family and we all had to come back to Alaska. Sorry. Leah? Leah? Are you okay?"

I listened, breathing hard. The sound of his voice soothed me.

"Leah, answer me. Look, I'm sorry. I know that you're mad I missed your party."

I sat frozen.

"Leah? Leah?"

I took a deep breath. "Why didn't you call me? I was worried sick. You can't do this to me again." The tears took over. I sobbed uncontrollably.

"Leah, I can't understand most of what you're saying, but I'm sorry. I'm going to have to stay in Alaska for a while."

That got my attention. "You're in Alaska?"

He didn't say anything.

I asked, "How long?"

"Longer than I want. Probably through Thanksgiving. Maybe

through Christmas."

My heart sank. How could I survive that long without my Z?

"Through Christmas? I'll miss you terribly, but I guess talking on the phone will have to do. We'll talk every day. Promise?"

"That's the bad part. Where I'm going in Alaska there are no cell connection towers. I won't be able to call you."

I heard him, but I didn't believe him. This was the twenty-first century.

I gasped. "No cell towers? That's impossible." I took in a deep breath. "What about the Internet? E-mails?"

He didn't answer for a while. "I'll try."

"I need you to tell Jorden all of this for Stella." The light of my life was leaving for maybe two months and now he wanted a favor. Stella and Jorden? Why would I care about Stella and Jorden at a time like this? Didn't he know how much I needed him? Wanted him? Couldn't live without him?

"Please come home." I couldn't help myself. He *had* to understand. "Come home to me now."

Another long pause. "I...I...I can't, Leah. I would if I could. It's a family thing."

"You could come home after the funeral. You know you could. YOU DON'T WANT TO COME HOME!" I screamed into the phone. It was crazy, but I couldn't help myself. I wept uncontrollably.

Another long pause. Was he listening to me cry? Did he want to hurt me?

Finally, he spoke. "I want to come back—more than you know."

I couldn't be consoled.

"I gotta go, Leah." He whispered.

"No! Please don't go!" I begged.

No response. Did he not live for me as I lived for him? If he did, how could he be so cruel? I finally asked the question that *had* to be asked. "You're coming back, right?'

White noise sounded. I stared at my phone. I freaked out. I called back. No answer. I called again. A computer voice came on the line and said that the phone was not able to take the call.

I called all night long. At five in the morning, I got a message that said the phone was no longer in service. I still called listening to the same automated message over and over again. I didn't sleep. I was wide awake when the alarm bell rang for me to get ready for school.

My swollen eyes stared back at me in the mirror. I didn't care. I looked horrible, but I felt much worse. I was lost. My life was over. I had turned fifteen and I had also ceased to exist. Z was gone. My reason for caring went with him. Despair surrounded me and I fell into its dark vat of doom. I was sinking and I knew I couldn't crawl out—ever. Blackness consumed me.

My body made it to school, my essence was with Z. He took me with him when he left—all that remained was a shell.

I went through the motions for the next few weeks. I wasn't eating or sleeping very well. My life didn't make much sense.

Jorden seemed to bounce right back after a short period of mourning. He was dazed when I told him that Stella wouldn't be back until maybe Christmas, but he was only sad for about a week. It wasn't long after that that he and Kelly started going out. I didn't understand how he could recuperate. How was that possible?

The weather emulated my mood. Florida had not had that many named hurricanes in a long while, but every week a new storm headed for our town. We'd put tape on the windows, buy supplies, fill the tub with water, and get mentally ready for the storm. When the hurricanes weren't coming, there were major thunderstorms. People commented that they couldn't remember the last time they saw the sun. The sunshine in my life had disappeared. My soul's essence felt dark and gloomy, exactly like the sky.

Heath had been great. He helped me every day with my weightlifting. He tried to lift my spirits with funny stories. Each day I got a little stronger physically, but inside I was still a wreck. I must have projected complete and utter defeat. Even Constance and her friends left me alone. Guess it wasn't much fun to pick on someone who was trounced on as bad as I was.

I pulled out my notebook to compose an essay assigned from English class. I started writing a story about my time with Z. I felt a little better. I decided to write how I felt every night. I tried to get better. I knew he would come back, I just knew he would. I had to survive until he did.

Sometimes I would sit and stare at his window across the street. I'd shut my eyes and imagine him. I'd have pretend conversations in my mind with him. I hugged the pillow with his scent. I wouldn't let my mother wash the pillowcase. His smell faded as the weeks went by. It was hard, but as his scent faded, my ability to be me started coming back. I fought hard to keep him with me. I didn't want to forget; I didn't want him to fade. I knew I would never ever feel that way again.

The holidays came and went. I put on a face of enjoying the Thanksgiving and Christmas dinners and opening presents. I cheered for the New Year, but my heart wasn't in it. My happiness and hope for the future was in Alaska.

My joy, like Z, had vanished.

In January, I knew in my heart he wasn't coming back.

The day the rental sign stood in his yard, I knew it was time. I sat in my room and stared at the necklace sitting on top of my dresser. I'd worn his anklet every day.

I had to try to pull myself out of this deep despair. Every time I looked at the anklet or felt it rub my ankle, I thought of him. It was time. I unhooked the anklet and kissed it before I placed it in my treasure box along with the poems, notes, and the chocolate candy. I put the ruby necklace back on.

It was cold outside and I felt cold inside. Fifteen could not be the end of everything. I found an old journal. I read a couple of entries about how I wanted to be a doctor. I couldn't remember the person who had written that entry. I had lost her. I had been so consumed by Z that I had lost myself. Our hearts had been intimate. Like the definition. We had been warmly close. He had been my whole world and when he went away, I allowed me, the real me, to go away too.

The day that sign went up in his yard, I knew. It was time for me, the real me, the me inside, to come back.

That Saturday, I walked down the stairs. Mom sat watching television.

"Whatcha watching?"

Mom jerked her head around, startled at first, then teared up, before she hugged me so tight I couldn't breathe. "I've been so worried about you. We all have." Then she let go and smiled. "I'm watching a movie. A comedy. Wanna watch with me?"

"I could use a laugh right now." I sat down with my mom and we laughed at the funny parts together. That day I found a little bit of Leah. I vowed I would never feel that much for someone again. No one would ever get that close. I would never let anyone hurt me like Z hurt me. I didn't know if I would be able to keep that promise, but I was sure going to try.

Chapter 14

The next day at school, the old group caught up with me and Kelly said, "We're going to the lake house this weekend." She had repeatedly asked me to go with her and Jane almost every week since Z had left. Today was no exception. "You wanta go?"

"Who all's going?" I looked at her squarely in the face. She was so taken aback by my response she froze.

Clay took his arm from around Jane's shoulder and answered for them all. "I think it's me, Jane, Kelly, and of course Jorden."

"I'll be odd man out." I said thinking *Kelly and Jorden, Jane and Clay, Leah and who?*

"We could invite some other people or maybe one other person?" Clay offered.

"No, that's all right. One thing at a time." I glanced at Kelly. "I'll come if you don't think I'll be too much of a drag."

"Not at all." Kelly smiled. The whole group flashed joyful knowing glances at each other. Gosh, if only I could make myself this happy.

"We could spend the night." Kelly grabbed my hand and Jane's. "Just like old times."

"That sounds nice." I really meant it. I wished it could be like old times, but my life was broken into two parts. Before Z and After Z. I wanted to get a little of "Before Z" back. I had been happy then, although now it was tough to remember.

After that, my focus started to come back and I began to set goals again.

I'd always wanted to be a doctor. Our biology class was scheduled to dissect this term. Exciting stuff! Something about seeing how the human body worked tantalized me. The miracle of life and how everything in the human body works together fascinated me. Instead of books about reading people's minds and psychic stuff, my borrowed books from the library consisted of titles about the heart and its mechanics, the anatomy of man, and nutrition and its place in medicine. The passion I felt for Z would be redirected into pursuing my life's work.

That decision gave me a happiness I hadn't felt in a long time.

One afternoon, I took an extended look at my reflection in the mirror. "Mom, can I get something new done with my hair this weekend? I need a new look."

Mom didn't hesitate. "We can go right now and see if they can fit you in. Do you have an idea of what you want? Let's get you a new outfit too."

"On a school night?" I asked.

"Why not?" She wrote a quick note to the family and grabbed her purse.

We walked out the door. My heart skipped a beat. There were cars across the street along with a moving van.

Mom grabbed my hand and led me to the car. "Renters. They have young children, three and five, I think."

"How long are they renting?" I asked, but put up my hand before she could answer. "Never mind."

Mom nodded as if she could read my mind. At the beauty shop, I opted for some layers and highlights. I had worn my hair straight and long for as long I could remember. I had them cut it just below my shoulders. I stared in the mirror. The highlights made my locks shine and Mom even bought me some hair products. Next, we went to the mall and stopped at the cosmetics counter. The lady adorned my face with makeup. I smashed my lips together spreading the gloss all over my lips. I liked it.

"I look older—maybe sixteen." I studied my image and my mom laughed. We bought mascara and lip-gloss.

At the department store, we picked out a few outfits, some off-season I wouldn't be able to wear till it warmed up a bit. Mom insisted on a teal fitted sweater and grey pants. "You've lost some weight." Mom commented, as we had to go a couple of sizes down.

"Maybe so." Despite the weight loss, I liked what I saw in the mirror. I looked happy. I just wanted to feel happy inside.

Astrid, Heath's sister, walked into the store as Mom made the purchases. "Buy anything good?"

"A few things." I pulled them out and showed her.

"For anything special?" She held my pants to her waist.

"Some of us are going to Kelly's lake house this weekend." I smiled.

Astrid put the pants back in the bag. "We're going too. We have a house there. Maybe we'll see you." She added, "I'm getting a dress for the Valentine's Dance in a few weeks."

We walked out of the store and Mom said, "Why don't we get you a new dress?"

I shot her a look. "For the Valentine's Dance that I'm not going to?"

Mom shook her head. "No, not for anything special but just to have a new dress. There's a place that just opened. It's a consignment shop. Let's see if we can find some good vintage wear. Besides, I wanted to check it out anyway."

I knew she really wanted to go, so I agreed. I didn't have to worry about seeing any of my friends in any of the outfits from that store. They wouldn't be caught dead in a consignment shop. Some people were weird about wearing used clothing. I liked vintage. Each piece of clothing had its own story. Wearing a piece with history appealed to me. Flipping through the racks, Mom saw it first— the prettiest red dress.

"It's the perfect shade of red for you." Mom gushed as she plucked it out. "You have to try it on."

It really looked like it was made for me. There was no talking my mom out of it once she saw it on me so now I had an outfit for this weekend, and a red Valentine's dress for a dance I had no plans to attend. I smiled at the irony. All dressed up and no place to go.

Spending the night was more pleasurable than I thought. I'd missed the girls. I thought it would be hard to listen to them go on and on about their boyfriends, but surprisingly it wasn't. I was happy for them. They had found a couple of the good guys, even if one of the guys was my brother.

"Have you ever told Clay you love him?" Kelly asked Jane.

Jane sat, pensive, on the floor beside the bed. "No. I'm not sure if I know what love is."

Kelly agreed. "Love seems like something you ought to save for the right person."

Had Z and I ever said we loved each other? I retraced our conversations. No, I didn't think we ever had. Somehow, that made me feel better. Maybe in some small way I'd saved a piece of my heart. That little piece wasn't destroyed. I silently scolded myself for thinking of Z.

I'd known Kelly and Jane forever and it was easy to fall back into finishing each other's thoughts and sentences. I felt more right then than I'd felt in months.

The next morning, I heard the banging first. I opened the curtain and there was Jorden beating on the window.

Kelly rolled out of bed and slammed back on the window. "C'mon—give us a minute to wake up. Come in through the sliding door in the back. We'll be out in a flash."

We took turns doing the two-minute shower and getting dressed. I threw on jeans and the new teal sweater.

"We made a bonfire in the pit! Hurry up!" Jorden raced down to the lakeside. There was a large fire blazing.

"We need marshmallows." Kelly announced and headed back to the house.

"The breakfast of champions!" Jane giggled.

"Astrid's coming. She just came out on their porch." Jorden glanced over at me.

I stared over to see what my twin was seeing. "Heath's coming too. Did you invite him?"

Jane perked up. "What are you guys talking about? I don't see anything except the lake."

I lifted my finger to point across the lake, but stopped and put my hand down and glanced at Jorden out of the corner of my eye.

Jane continued. "How can you see Heath's house? It's a couple of miles across the lake."

She stared at me and I peeked at Jorden trying to read his face.

Jorden locked his gaze on me. "Jane, could you go and get me a soda?"

"Now?"

Jorden smiled at her. "Yes, now. I'd really appreciate it."

Jane trotted off toward the house, mumbling under her breath about how she wasn't anyone's slave.

Jorden lifted his head staring back at me, our gaze still locked. "She's gone." He leaned over and whispered. "You can see the people in the house across the lake too, can't you?"

Chapter 15

"**Y**es!" I squealed.

He yelped. "I can and you can!"

I jumped up and hugged my brother. "I can't believe it."

He jerked me so hard I thought he would pull my arms off. "We need to talk."

I spotted Kelly and Jane coming down the trail. I said, "Later."

I was so relieved that I was going to be able to talk to someone else about all of the things that were happening to me. I think besides what I obviously missed about Z, I missed having a confidante, a person that I could tell my most intimate secrets to with no judgment. A long time ago, Jorden and I had shared everything.

Heath and Astrid showed up a few minutes later. Heath had a couple of poles. "We're fishing, right?"

I grabbed a pole. "I'll fish."

Heath smiled. "Glad you decided to join the living again. You've been missed."

We spent the afternoon fishing or playing at fishing. Jane caught the most and Clay accused her of sweet-talking the fish. She laughed so much she said she almost made herself pee. We decided to fry our catch. We needed some potato chips so Heath offered to drive to the store. I decided to tag along.

"So what kind of chips do we want?" Heath pulled a few bags down to study their labels.

"I like them all." I pulled a couple more bags down. "You pick."

Ultimately, we got way too many, six sacks.

"Anything else?" He glanced around. "I'm paying."

"In that case, have you ever heard of S'mores?" I led him over to the aisle with the marshmallows and threw two bags in the cart.

"Great idea." He tossed in some graham crackers.

I found the chocolate candy bars and grabbed a couple of packages more than we needed. I lifted my eyebrow and made a funny face. "For later, I love chocolate."

He chuckled and added another box of candy bars. "Me too. I think that's everything we need."

We made our way out to his jeep. Rugged and humongous, painted black with silver trim, it looked like it was right off a big game hunter show from the *Discovery Channel*. I guessed that was how it was when your parents have a lot of money.

He opened the jeep door for me. "I wanted to ask you something. And feel free to say no. It won't hurt my feelings or anything."

I slid into the front seat. "What?"

He shut the door and loaded the groceries in the back before he climbed in the driver's seat. He finally spit it out. "Would you go to the Valentine's Dance with me?"

Surprised, I hesitated for a moment, and then answered, "Sure. Why not?" I smiled. "Actually, I just gotta new dress. It's red. It'll be perfect."

Heath's face lit up. I could have gone through the whole scenario of saying—*well if we just go as friends*. But I decided to start doing what I wanted to do. Heath was my weightlifting buddy. He told me jokes when I was at my lowest. He was a nice guy, and a nice guy was just what I needed.

"Heath and I are going to the Valentine's Dance together." I blurted out when we got back to the group. Total silence. It was a little awkward so I added. "And we also bought stuff for S'mores." Cheers erupted. We all laughed.

Heath dropped Jorden and me by our house late that night.

Jorden shut the door behind me. "You better come to my room so we can talk. Not so many ears."

I nodded. I knew who he was talking about—Terra.

I followed him to his room and he shut the door. His room was a mess. Books and clothes littered the floor. I shoved things out of the way with my foot to create a path. I wasn't sure where to sit and finally spied the only uncluttered spot, his desk chair. I grabbed it and plopped down.

He pushed some video games off his bed and sat on the corner. "Spill."

I gushed like a waterfall that had been dammed forever. I told him all about *The Voice* and the things that I had searched for— the mind reading and the psychic powers I thought I had. I shared about being able to see, hear, and smell things so strong that it should be impossible.

"I'm not scared about all of it, just confused."

He listened without speaking. I took a breath after my oration. Then he confessed he'd had a lot of the same incidences. His experiences had started after Christmas and he hadn't told anybody. He had had a heightened sense of smell and taste and sight— all of the things I had described.

"I missed you."

"Me too." He socked me playfully on the shoulder. "Seriously, we're twins. We should tell each other everything."

I hugged him. "We will from now on."

Chapter 16

I'd spent the better part of an hour getting ready for the Valentine's Dance. Doing and redoing my hair and trying on four pairs of shoes, finally opting for peep-toe nude stilettos. Accessories gave me such a headache, I gave up—just went with my everyday wear— gold hoops and my ruby necklace. I hadn't tried to put together an ensemble in a while, but for some unknown reason I cared about my appearance tonight.

"How do I look?" I asked Jane and Kelly.

"Great!" Kelly twirled in her pink off-shoulder dress and strappy silver shoes. "How 'bout me?"

Jane swished her lavender skirt. "We all look good. I'm glad we decided to get ready together. I can't believe that Heath is getting a limo."

"Me neither." I pulled the clasp on my necklace to the back. "It'll be fun though— all of us going together."

"Yeah, it will." Kelly grabbed her clutch. "I hear the doorbell. Let's go."

I brushed my lips with a bit more gloss and followed the other two down the stairs. The three guys—Clay, Heath, and Jorden— waited on us.

Heath smiled, handsome in his black tuxedo with a bowtie. "You're beautiful."

The compliment made me smile. "Thanks."

Clay stumbled over to stand by Heath. "Yeah.. yeah...you all look great." He fumbled at his shirt, pulling it out from the band and

95

nervously stuffing it in again.

Jorden finally stood and ambled over to the other two, fiddling with his tie. "Mom, my bowtie came undone."

Clay struck a pose. "You shoulda got a clip-on like mine."

Everybody laughed which lightened the mood. Mom fixed Jorden's bowtie and took pictures from every angle possible until we escaped.

Heath jumped in the back of the limousine and shut the door. "Finally!"

"Wow, this has everything." Jane clinked some champagne glasses together. "Are we going to drink?"

Heath pulled out a bottle. "Sure why not? It's non-alcoholic champagne."

The boys pumped their fists and whooped. Clay found the controls and music blared as we sipped our non-alcoholic champagne. Jane, Kelly, and I opened the roof, squeezed out to wave with one hand while holding our hair with the other so as not to muss it up, and laughed.

"I've always wanted to do that." I sat back down.

Heath scooted close to me. "I have a Valentine's present for you." He retrieved a small, beautifully wrapped box out of his pocket.

I opened my purse and handed him a tiny box of candy. "I brought you one too. Happy Valentine's Day."

"Great." He opened the candy, tossed one of the chocolates in his mouth, and mumbled, "Now yours."

I opened the present carefully so as not to break the bow. It was an opal ring. "My birthstone!"

"I hope you like it." He slid it on my finger. It fit perfectly.

I pulled the ring halfway off. "It's beautiful, but it's too much."

"Leah, I want you to have it and I won't take no for an answer." He glanced at me and added, "It's a friendship ring. You are my friend, right?"

I really did want the ring. The fire opal was beautiful. I had seen a few in the stores. In the right light, the white stone exploded with color.

I gazed at his hopeful eyes. "Of course I'm your friend. I love it. Thank you." I leaned over and kissed him lightly on the cheek.

He beamed. "Happy Valentine's Day."

All kinds of papier-mâché hearts and flowers and cupids hung from the ceiling of the gym. Pink and white balloons lined the entranceway. Heath and I struck a pose by the heart-shaped entrance. A photographer had us stand in a couple of positions as his camera snapped.

The gang found a table and we put our stuff down. A wild song played and we all went out on the floor to dance. We would stop every so often to catch our breath, get a drink, or sit for a minute. No one was dancing with anyone in particular. I was having a blast. For the first time in a long time, I didn't feel consumed with sadness.

Constance was dancing, with her jock flavor of the month. She danced by me and whispered, "So you finally moved on. You seem to have no problem getting guys to fall all over you." Then she smiled mischievously. "Well that is, all except Z who musta seen the light, since he dumped your butt." I didn't give her the satisfaction of a reaction, but I knew the gloves were off and my reprieve had ended.

Someone requested a slow song. We were all out on the dance floor and everyone paired up. Heath and I were left, standing close together. He put his arms out and I moved closer, putting one hand on his shoulder and my other hand in his. We swayed to the music and he held me away from him a little distance. I started feeling comfortable and I moved a little closer. I finally put my head on his chest. Even in my stilettos, I didn't come but to his chest. I peeked up at him. I could feel my face soften. He sure was nice.

He kissed the top of my head. "You know I'm crazy about you. Have been from the first day I saved you from the truck."

I didn't know how to respond. I started to say something, but someone grabbed my arm and pulled us apart.

Chapter 17

"**G**randma!" Heath yelled at the withered white-haired lady standing in front of us.

Grandma gasped. "She wears the bloodstone."

"What are you talking about?" Heath glanced at me, confused.

"She is not for you." His grandmother grabbed his arm. She touched my arm. "I'm sorry."

Heath held his grandmother at arm's length and mouthed. "Sorry."

He tried to lead his grandmother off the dance floor. "Grandma, where are Mom and Dad? Did they bring you?"

I walked beside them. "What is the bloodstone?" I asked his grandmother. "I've heard that before from someone."

His grandmother stopped dead in her tracks. Her eyes almost shut as if to gauge my response. "You have? Where?"

"I...I don't remember..." I wasn't going to admit it was a dream. "I really don't know." Closer to the truth.

Heath's grandmother's demeanor changed from attacker to friend as Heath's parents walked up. She grabbed me in one arm and Heath in the other. "Forgive an old woman."

Mr. Bolcan ran towards her. "What's going on, Mom? I thought you were going to the bathroom."

"Sorry, I saw our Heath here man-handling..." the grandmother began.

"I wasn't..." Heath started, but his grandmother put her hand over his mouth.

Grandma continued. "Sorry, I meant to say pawing."

Heath tried to interrupt, but Grandma started again. "Anyway, I wanted to meet Heath's girlfriend."

"Grandma." Heath sighed and pointed at me. "This is Leah... Leah Skye."

"Skye...yes..." A strange smile made her eyes crinkle and her face softened. "Heath, I insist, you must bring your beautiful girl to the house tomorrow for dinner." Then she peered back at me. "I want to show her some things."

Heath shifted uncomfortably. "What—my baby pictures?"

"Something like that." Grandmother smiled.

Heath's mother said, "Of course, Heath. Bring your girl to dinner tomorrow night." She smiled at me. "We'd love to get to know any of Heath's friends."

Heath's parents led his grandmother away.

"Wow, maybe we ought to sit down so I don't paw you anymore." Heath laughed nervously as we walked over to the table. "Old people sometimes get a little confused."

I touched his hand. "You weren't pawing, but maybe we ought to slow down a bit. I can't take another—"

He finished my sentence. "—broken heart?"

I nodded. "I'm really not ready."

"I wouldn't break your heart. You're all I think of." He glanced down and his face flushed. "We can take our time. I know you've been hurt...hurt badly... but your life's not over. Give living a chance. You might enjoy it again."

I touched his face. "You're really sweet." I felt better than I had felt in a really long time. Maybe I was on the mend. "Let's just keep it a friendship."

He added, "For now."

We hardly sat down the rest of the dance. I'd look over every once in a while and see Heath's grandmother watching. It was a bit eerie. I danced with Clay and even with Jorden. Heath danced with all the girls. He tried to get out of dancing with Constance, but she could be quite persuasive and Heath was not the kind of person who would make a scene. She gloated the whole time. There was absolutely nothing about her that I liked.

The limousine stopped at my house after it had dropped everyone else off and Heath walked me to the door. He took my hand and kissed it lightly. "Guess you're coming to dinner tomorrow. Pick you up around six. Okay?"

"That sounds fine." I tiptoed up to hug him and whispered in his ear. "Thanks for a great night. I really needed it."

When I walked in the foyer, I saw Mom and Dad were waiting up. Mom asked, "Did you have a nice time?"

"I really did." It was the truth.

The next morning, I decided to go outside. Jorden was playing basketball with the hoop in the driveway. I threw a few with him. We started a game of H.O.R.S.E. Then Blue stopped working on his car and joined us. Then we added Terra and Mom and Dad.

"Let's walk down to the park to play full court." Dad suggested.

We had a great game of three on three. Mom, Terra, and Blue against Jorden, Dad, and me. It was close, but my team squeaked by and won in the end.

I hadn't even noticed someone watching us until we were finished.

It was Stone from the first of the year. "Hey, remember me?"

"Oh yeah." I wiped sweat off my face with my hand. "I'm a little sweaty. Sorry."

Stone grabbed my hand and held onto it. He closed his eyes. "Please be careful."

"Careful about what, playing basketball?" I tried to pull my hand away but he held onto it and said, "Danger is coming and you need to be strong."

Jorden dribbled the ball up to us. "You okay, sis?"

Stone released my hand and shook his head as if he had broken out of a trance. "Hey, remember me? Stone from the first of the year."

"Y... yes." I stammered, frowning. "You just said that."

"I did?" He brushed his hair back. "Did I say anything else?"

"No," I lied. "See ya. Let's go, Jorden." I was ready to get home. This had been the weirdest two days. First, the grandmother, and now this. Was the message for me? Why did Stone say it and not remember? If the message was true, why did Stone deliver it? Why didn't he remember what he said? What kind of danger could I be in? It was all so confusing.

I cleaned up and got ready to go to Heath's house. I was looking forward to it. At precisely six that evening, the doorbell rang. *Prompt, I like that.*

Heath showed me around his estate and it *was* an estate—a mansion on the lake. We toured the gardens, projection room, tennis and basketball courts, a bowling alley, and a three-hole golf course.

I joked. "Does your Dad own all of Hawaii?"

Heath laughed. "Only the best parts."

I couldn't tell if he meant it or not.

Heath's Mom and Dad joined us for dinner out on the veranda, with a chef who served a meal of fried shrimp, cheese grits, and hush puppies.

Heath's grandmother joined us late. "There is Leah... Leah Skye. Hello, dear. I don't think I formally introduced myself. I'm Jewell Bolcan, but you call me Grandma Jewell. Everyone does."

I grinned and nodded.

She continued. "I want you to see something I've been working on—after we finish eating."

Heath interrupted. "We'll be glad to."

"No, just us girls, Heath." Grandma Jewell glanced at me. "Okay with you Leah, Leah Skye?"

"S...sure." I stuttered.

"Then it's settled. Let's eat."

Dinner conversation morphed to a more animated and lively tone centering on school, the town, and Hawaii.

After dinner, Grandma Jewell waved her hand for me to follow.

101

I excused myself and trailed her up some stairs to a room way in the back. It was full of old books and smelled musty. She motioned for me to sit on a cushioned chair. Dust flew up as I plopped down. Did she ever let anyone in to clean?

Grandma Jewell carefully pulled out an age-worn book from under the coffee table, adorned with a large hand-drawn star on the front cover, and opened it in front of me. "I think it's about time you found out about your ancestors."

Chapter 18

"**M**y ancestors?" I stared at Grandma. "How could you know about my ancestors?"

Her face blanked and I relaxed. What could it hurt to humor an old woman and listen to a few wild tales?

She seemed to sense my skepticism. "I really need you to listen and take me seriously."

I nodded and put on the most serious façade I could muster. "I'm listening."

She opened the first page of the book to a drawing of a star and a family tree chart. "There was a prophecy told thousands of years ago."

Curious, I glanced at the drawing—families of tribes?

She continued. "These were the ancient ones. We are descendants of these tribes. Your and my ancestors were all located on an island off the coast of what is today the state of California."

I stopped her. "Yours? And my ancestors?"

She patted my hand. "Let me tell it."

I nodded and gazed at the old book. It was so dilapidated I hoped it didn't disintegrate in her hands.

She carefully turned the page to a map that resembled the west coast of America.

I asked, "Where in California?"

She pointed to an island.

I conjured up a remembrance of geography. "You mean Alcatraz?"

"Yes, it's known as Alcatraz today." She ran her finger over the map. "See, there it is."

I turned the page back to check the front of the book. "When was this written?"

There was a hand-written list of names and Grandma Jewell was the last entry on the page.

Grandma Jewell answered, "This book consists of collections from our ancestors, maps, pictures, and more recently, photographs. The book has been passed down generation after generation. I've added to it; generations after me will add to it."

She pinched the last few pages together upright between her fingers. "I don't know the exact time that the writings started. At first, stories passed verbally from generation to generation, but most of those stories and rules have now been recorded."

She stopped and took a breath. "Goodness, I'm jumping ahead of myself. All in good time, dear."

She flipped back to the first page and gestured to the hand-drawn map. "In the first days..."

I interrupted. "First days like when? Dinosaur times?"

She smiled. "No dear. From the etchings and verbal stories passed down the beginning was determined to be somewhere around 100 A.D." She stopped and glanced up at the ceiling. "That was a long time ago."

Then she focused back on the book. "Anyway, in the first days we were joined together. Our tribes communicated through drums. Alcatraz, or as it was known then Island of the Star, was the place where the high Priest and Priestess of each clan lived."

She spread her hands outward. "During this time there were five tribes. Star, Sky, Volcano, Water and Island. At that time, their powers were strong. They were named for the lifeblood of the world. In order to keep the families strong, marriages took place between people of different tribes."

"What kind of powers?" I interrupted. "What do you mean by marriages between tribes?"

"Powers, we'll get to later on, but marriages." She held our both palms and pointed to one hand. "If this hand is the Star tribe and this…" She pointed to her other hand. "…is the Sky tribe. Then they can join together." She placed her palms flat against each other. "This made both tribes stronger. A Star family member could marry a Sky Clan and so forth. The men ruled and would always stay with their original tribe and the women would join their mate's tribe. Children of their union would be members of the man's family. A Priest's mate would become the Priestess of his clan."

She put her hands down and flipped the page—more pictures and drawings of tribes. I had lots of questions and it was hard not to blurt them out. I struggled to control my curiosity because this was all so fascinating and I wanted to hear more.

She gently rubbed her finger over the page. "For many years the five clans lived in harmony."

I interrupted, "Do the five points have anything to do with the star on the front?"

She flipped the book to the front cover. "Very observant. The five point star had everything to do with the clans. Five points of the star—five tribes. You are a very smart girl. Be patient."

"Sorry." I traced the star with my finger before she turned it back.

She continued, "After the time of peace…" She looked up from the book. "I guess you want to know when this was too." I nodded and she continued. "I calculated around 600 A.D. That is when the trouble started. A great warrior of the Volcano Clan became enamored with the chosen mate for the Priest of the Star tribe. The chosen Priestess was a member of the Sky family and was also smitten by the great Volcano Clan warrior who was not supposed to be her mate. The two were in love, but not chosen for one another. A marriage ceremony was arranged for the Star priest and his Sky bride. But the Volcano warrior was powerful and threatened violence if she married the Priest. He claimed her as his wife going against tribal rules."

I remembered my premonition. "Arranged marriage."

Grandma Jewell repeated. "Yes, arranged marriage. It was an accepted tradition during this time. This one act caused a great dispute among the five clans. A power struggle ensued which resulted in a long and bloody civil war. The Volcano and Star groups fought. The other two tribes conspired to kill the Priestess in an attempt to stop the fighting, but the Sky Clan protected its daughter. Attempts on her life failed, but set in motion the demise of the five points. During this time, there were great battles. One such battle wiped out the men of the Sky kin. The Sky Clan Priestess escaped and went into hiding. The rest of the women and children of the Sky people were divided among the other four tribes. Because of the destruction of the Sky tribe, the five points no longer formed a star."

I studied the drawing. "They lost their power?" This was my guess based on art depicting the star breaking apart.

She opened her fist and waved her fingers wide apart. "Yes. They fractured and the destruction of the Sky clan caused their powers to disappear."

I asked again, "What kind of powers?"

She ran her finger over the broken star. "I promise I will tell you about the powers later, but you must understand the beginning. Be patient."

I sighed. "Okay."

She continued, "During this time, a curse came upon the Island of the Star. Great hardships in weather and famine made their idyllic life unbearable. With new people invading their territory, the remaining four clans met and decided the only way to survive was to separate. They built great ships and set sail, relying on fate to show them the way. Each clan was to pass down their past stories and record new histories for future generations. A historical tablet depicting rules, creeds, ceremonies, and other descriptions of the ancient ones' cultures was included along with a prophecy. The prophecy was to be read during a solar eclipse just before solstice in the fire sign month. This happened on December 14, 1955. It is believed that all of the clans opened their books simultaneously to read the prophecy."

"A Prophecy?" This story was getting more and more interesting.

She slowly turned the page, uncovering an ornate series of drawings. "This is a pictorial rendition drawn to summarize the prophecy."

"See." Her hand passed over a drawing of four points of the broken star. "We are all disconnected. Writings support a rebirth when all five clans would gather again." She ran her hand to the end of the page where the star was connected again.

She rubbed the book. "Do you want to know why I'm telling you all of this?"

"Yes."

She waved her hand across the page of drawings. "It is told that as the rebirth begins, there would be a descendant of the Sky family who would be able to hear words that were not spoken, would be able to see things from a far distance, and this person would inherit other powers and do great things. The commencement of this person's gifts would signal the beginning of the prophecy."

My breath labored nervously as my heart pounded.

She paused and turned to a map of the world drawn on the next page. "Watch. After the Sky Clan was no more and the tribes separated, the Star Clan went to the great north." She marked a dot on the map with a pen at North Alaska. "The Volcano went to the far west and settled on an island." She marked a dot at Hawaii. "The Island went to the east to a part of the Aleutian Islands and the Water Clan settled near Manitoba in Canada." She marked both those points. "Where the lines crossed where we were first together was our original island, now known as Alcatraz. The new place—where the rebirth would happen—would be at the last point."

She spread the page so the map laid down flat. "Look." She drew a line from each of the dots, Alaska to Hawaii up to Canada, over to the Aleutian Islands and brought the last line to cross Alcatraz and it ended up in Berry, Florida.

"It forms a large star across the world." Her voice quivered with excitement as she talked. "It ends in Berry."

She grinned at me. "I always thought the chosen one would be male, but then I saw the bloodstone…"

"What are you talking about?" I jumped up. "You think I'm this long lost girl come back to save some ancient clan." I shook my head. "I'm just...me. Nothing special. I'm not a descendant of anything as interesting as all of this."

She took my necklace in her hand. "You *are* special. You wear the bloodstone."

I pulled the necklace out of her hand. "I don't understand what wearing this ruby has to do with anything. It was my grandmother's."

She turned a few pages in the hand-written book. There it was—an exact drawing of my ruby. "The bloodstone was the mark of the Sky Clan. It is written that the bloodstone will find its way into a new one's hands—the one who will signal the beginning of the prophecy. That's you. You are the heir to the prophecy."

I stopped her. "My mother had this necklace when I was born. She wore it. Why wouldn't she be the heir to the prophecy?" *Why was I trying to drag my mother into this madness?*

"You don't understand. There is a particular time that all of this will happen. The stone may have had many owners before you, but things have started happening now *because* it is in your hands. Timing makes a difference."

"Look, I'll show you. The bloodstone is given to the heir and then and only then do the clans start gathering in the final leg of the star." She went back to the drawing. "The final point of the star ends in Berry."

"All right. For argument's sake say, I believed all of the hocus-pocus. What clans are gathering? I'm not seeing a bunch of clans gathering in Berry."

"The head of the Volcano Clan started this school didn't he?" She turned the page. "There was a family tree with all of the Volcano Clan and how they had changed their name to Bulkan when they moved to the Islands. *Bulkan* is the Filipino translation for volcano, and that eventually morphed to *Bolcan*.

"Heath," I murmured, staring at his family pictures in the book.

"Okay so *your* clan is here." I closed the book. "So what?"

"We aren't the only clans who have come." She opened the

book up again and I recognized a picture.

"Stone?" I shivered. "I know him."

"His family is from the Water Clan. Look." She turned the page. "They were originally named Maree which means water or pool in French, an influence from the Canadian French. They eventually changed their name to the literal meaning, Poole."

I'd never heard his last name.

She showed me the page with the Island Clan from the Aleutian Islands. Their name had been changed to many translations for island and ended up Otok, a Croatian translation. I glanced at the pictures of the last entries. Students I recognized from Berry Academy.

"Let's say I buy all of this. Island, Volcano, Water...and if we are Sky. That's still only four clans...four points of the star. " I flipped through the pages. I stopped. Why hadn't I connected it before?

On the last page of pictures of the Star Clan history—now called Starre—was a photograph of Z.

Chapter 19

"Z." I outlined his face in the picture with my fingers.

Grandma pushed my hand away and shut the book. "This boy is not meant for you."

"I know. He left me. Now you're just being mean!" I stood up, towering over her.

She patted the air in a quieting motion. "Calm down. The boy is not the eldest son."

"Why would that matter?"

She thumbed to a page entitled Clan Laws. "It is not the clan way. An eldest boy must go with an eldest girl. Younger children must wait their turn."

A knock sounded at the door and it swung open. "Grandma?" Heath walked in the room and Grandma shut her book quietly and carefully slid it on the floor in front of the coffee table.

"Do you know about these—?" I started.

"Of course he knows that I have been sharing our old photos." Grandma slyly pushed the book under the coffee table. She quickly opened an album showing a smiling Heath riding a pony when he was about eight or nine years old.

Heath backed out the door. "Aw, Grandma."

I frowned. Maybe she was some crazy old lady after all. I would do some searching on my own before I blew the whistle on this nut case. What if she has a touch of dementia and made this entire elaborate story up? All I knew was that she didn't want me to tell Heath. I decided to play along. True or not, I wanted to know more.

"We're almost through with our visit. We'll be there in just a few minutes," She called out to Heath as he pulled the door shut and disappeared.

Grandma grasped my hands. "I've confused you. I know you have a lot of questions. All will be answered in time. Let what I have told you sink in. Then come back and I'll tell you more."

She asked, "What do you aspire to do with your life?"

"Just to make it clear—I'm not your prophecy. I plan on being a doctor." I meant it too.

She smiled. "A healer might be your destiny. I want to tell you one thing before you leave tonight." She led me to the door.

"Because there has been a gathering of the clans, there has been a shift in the stars and sky. Some do not want the Sky Clan to rise again. They don't want the heir to make the prophecy come true. Great gifts and powers will be bestowed upon the rightful heirs. Some want those gifts for themselves. If this prophecy does not come to pass, it is their belief the powers will be given to them. Competition makes wars. Be aware and keep all of this to yourself."

Her tone frightened me.

"I cannot tell you who these people are," she said, "Only that there is unrest. Be careful. Tell no one of our conversation. The only thing protecting your identity is that we have always thought the prophecy heir would be a male and not a female. Signs of the prophecy coming true are all around us." She peered at me. "And you have something to do with all of that. Let's see if we can find out what. There are so many interpretations, it is hard to know the true path."

I nodded, half-believing what she said. "Yeah, I know I have nothing to do with all this hocus pocus."

She touched the ruby around my neck. "Your gifts are developing."

I jumped. My reaction gave me away. No way to hide now.

"You've noticed a change all ready. Good." She smiled knowingly. "Your gift of senses will grow. You are a child in that regard. You have much growing to do. Hide your gifts. Be careful, Sky daughter." She opened the door and we walked out. "We'll talk soon.

You have given me great hope." She grinned, reached up, and patted me on the shoulder. "Goodnight, dear."

My mind swirled with all she had told me. I saw Heath. I didn't think I'd be able to hide my distress.

I grabbed my stomach. "I don't feel so good."

Heath walked over and held me up. Sweet guy.

"Was it looking at my baby pictures?" He chuckled. He always tried to cheer me up.

"Probably just a virus," I lied. "You better take me home. I don't want to get sick all over your floor."

I said a quick goodbye to his family. He helped me out to the car. I couldn't wait to get home and try to make sense out of all of this. Some kind of an heir? To what? I couldn't deny one truth about Z, Heath, and Stone. I was drawn to all three.

I hung out the window on the way home to complete the deception. Heath walked me to the door and made a quick getaway. I didn't blame him. I told him I might puke all over him more than once.

Mom met me at the door. "How'd dinner go?"

Maybe the lie would work here too. "I ate something that didn't agree with me. I don't feel so good. Okay if I go to bed? I'll tell you all about dinner in the morning."

Mom was going to be a little harder to get away from. "Maybe I should—" she started.

"Leave me alone, Grace. I think I'm going to throw up." I ran up the stairs, yelling back to her. "I'll lie down. I'll be all right. Just want to rest now okay? Please stay out of my business." I worked hard to sound like I did when I wanted her to butt out of my business.

"Okay." She yelled up the stairs. Good, she'd leave me alone for the night.

I scrunched in between the bed and the window and sat on the floor. I opened my laptop and searched for the clans. I scanned through the list, nothing of use to me. I put in *sky, Sky Clan, five point*, and *prophecy* for about a half an hour. One of the searches had the words "ancient folklore." I tried it. A long list. I added *sky*. Another list. I added *Sky Clan prophecy*. There it was!

The first part of the website contained an accounting of the Sky Clan. The site's source was a man who claimed to have infiltrated a clan and been taught their folklore, legends, and prophecies.

The words corroborated Grandma's story of the clans and their life on Alcatraz.

Legend has it that the five ancient clans were once powerful and enjoyed great wealth and comfort. It is not known how long they have been in existence. Historians place an uprising somewhere around the seventh century.

Stories handed down through generations trace this uprising to a single event when a clan member stole a bride from a rival clan setting in motion a series of events that signified their downfall. It was told that the Sky Priest, who was a trusting soul, agreed to meet with the elders of the other four clans to try to come to an agreement.

During this meeting, the other clans attacked and eradicated the Sky Clan's male population. The surviving women and children were dispersed amongst the other clans. The Sky Clan ceased to exist.

The remaining clans found their food supply drying up and constant barrages of earthquakes and storms threatened their homes and safety. Fearing they had enraged the gods, the other four clans agreed to live separate lives.

A surviving female sky clan member claimed to have been visited by a priestess with wings in a vision and told of an elaborate rebirth prophecy. This prophecy was verbally shared and passed down generation to generation until it was recorded in written word. The existence of these ancient clans would be kept secret from outsiders and clan historians would document their past and their future.

The books of this clan have been sought after, but never discovered. Richard Montfield, a journalist of the late 1880s, recorded this information from a dying man in 1884 in an Arizona tuberculosis hospital. The man died without identification or before he could tell Montfield about the prophecy.

Montfield brought this to life in a western fiction entitled "Sky Clan." These westerns are rare and only one copy is known to exist. It is owned by a Robert Lant.

I clicked on a section entitled Sky Clan's gifts.

The Sky Clan was known as the tribe who could hear, see, touch, and taste more than other people. A 1964 report gathered from an interview by a journalist, Robert Lant—

I stopped. Robert Lant again. I read some more.

—of John Longfeather, a man who claimed that members of the original Sky Clan could read people's thoughts—Longfeather reported Sky clan could hear what people were thinking about saying and had vision that could see the very bones inside a man, superhuman vision. All Sky Clan members reportedly died of Black Death around the sixth century. Lant found a western story from a writer entitled Sky Clan. Lant is still researching the ancient clans.

I searched Robert Lant. I found Robert Lant, an author of various books on ancient folklore. There was a webpage and an email address—worth a try.

Dear Mr. Lant,

You don't know me but I am very much interested in the folklore that centers on the tribesmen of Alcatraz. Specifically, The Island of the Star clan. Thanks in advance for your time and I look forward to hearing from you.

Sincerely,
Leah Skye

As I reviewed the words and sent off the email, my thoughts raced back to the book Grandma Jewell had shared. I thought of all of the pictures she'd shown me. I'm scared. I have to process all of this.

Then it happened, my lie became the truth. I went in the bathroom, squatted at the toilet, and puked my guts out.

Chapter 20

I slept fitfully that night and the rest of the week trying to understand all I had heard and read. I researched the Otoks. One Otok son was a junior at our school. The other boy was still in middle school. I even made a point to try to run into Stone before I went to the gym for dance class every day. No matter how hard I searched, I just couldn't find anything out of the ordinary about any of these people. I couldn't find anything out of the ordinary about me either—except maybe *The Voice* and the heightened senses. I had to admit that was unusual. Could there be others that are just like me trying to hide some kind of ability?

I checked my email daily, to hear from Mr. Lant. Finally on Friday, there it was.

Dear Ms. Skye,

Thanks for your interest in my writings. I'm sorry it took me so long to answer back. My assistant screens my emails. Your mention of the Island of the Star Clan perked my interest.

Please comment on the following:

A lesser-known fable suggests not all the Sky Clan were killed off and that one lone male of the Sky Clan along with his mate survived and began a new line that will rise again. The ancestors of that linage were rumored to reside in the United States. Another suggests that a warrior and a Sky Clan priestess escaped the plague.

I look forward to hearing back from you. Please reply to this email. It is my personal email and does not go through an assistant.

115

Sincerely,
Robert Lant

I responded.

Dear Mr. Lant,
I have heard this story.
Sincerely,
Leah Skye

I hit send, and then I looked in the mirror to hear or see something I wasn't supposed to. I tried to conjure up *The Voice.* No luck. The next day I received another email from Mr. Lant.

Dear Ms. Skye,

I would very much like to know where you heard the story. I have enclosed more information. Please let me know if you've heard of these.

An obscure prophecy was first reported in 1878 by Harold Alder, a gold miner. He unearthed an ancient stone while mining a tunnel on Alcatraz. He had the pictures that had been drawn on the stone deciphered. It illustrated a prophecy that the Sky Clan will rise to join the clans together in the 21st century. The ancient drawings and the origin of the drawings remain unknown. A rough translation of two symbols thought to say "Bloodstone" were found on one of the mangled, broken pieces. It is feared that the legend will forever be incomplete. With the stone's authenticity never established and the mystery never solved, the widely circulated story concluded that a prisoner of Alcatraz most likely left it as an elaborate hoax.

Sincerely,
Robert Lant

I wrote back that I'd heard about the bloodstone and went to bed.

That night I heard my email beep. It was two in the morning. I crawled out of bed to open the email.

Dear Ms. Skye,

I think we need to meet. See below. Do you know if this is true?

There are ancient books in existence with information about the Island of the Star.

Sincerely,

Robert Lant

It was late and I was tired, but I decided to send a short reply. I wanted to know the *real* story. I would ask my mom about a meeting tomorrow. I most likely knew what her answer would be, but I'd ask anyway.

Dear Mr. Lant,

I'll have to ask about meeting with you, but I can tell you for sure, there is at least one book.

Sincerely,

Leah Skye

I fell asleep. In the morning with the email still on my mind, I shot off another quick response to ask Mr. Lant where he was located. No reason to go through getting permission if he lived close enough that I could walk to meet him.

I was beginning to feel like my old self. Heath invited me and the rest of the gang, plus a few others to his house for a day of sports. He had everything we needed to play golf, tennis, ping-pong, cricket, and table games.

Heath picked me up around ten in the morning and we headed for his house. "Grandma wants you to start coming over to the house to read to her for an hour a week."

"Read her what?"

Heath turned into his driveway. "I don't know. I think she took a liking to you. My parents are supposed to call your parents to set a time weekly for you to do it. I thought it was crazy at first, but you know you could get community hours you need for scholarships for when you graduate." He knocked me in the shoulder playfully. "Reading to the elderly."

"I'll think about it." I glanced at him. "Is she going to be here today? I'll ask her about it."

After a few pleasantries, Heath's parents gathered their belongings.

I asked, "Are you leaving?"

"Yeah," Heath's father said. "We thought we'd let you young people have the house today."

"Is Grandma Jewell here?" I glanced up the stairs toward her room.

"She is, but she won't bother you. She did want to talk to you sometime today, Leah. Just go knock on her door." Heath's mother closed the door behind them.

I didn't waste any time. "Heath, I'm going to talk to her now so I can concentrate on the games. I really want to win." He grinned and I took off up the stairs.

I knocked lightly. "Grandma."

"Come in, child." She was sitting on her overstuffed chair. "I've wanted to talk to you."

"So I heard." She motioned for me to sit down on an adjacent chair.

"I think we should start your lessons." She patted my hand.

"Lessons? What lessons?'

"Oh." She laughed to herself. "Sorry. I'm an old woman. I forget sometimes what I have told people. You are...how old are you?"

"Fifteen."

"Perfect." She pulled out the old book. "The age of sixteen is when your abilities are supposed to start developing. Since your gifts have already started manifesting themselves that means you will have very powerful skills."

"I'm not sure I'm buying into all of this mumbo jumbo."

"I don't expect you to, dear." She smiled. "At least not at first, but aren't you curious to see if this old woman knows what she is talking about? What's the worst that could happen? You will spend an hour a week giving an old woman one of her final—" she coughed a bit. She was hamming it up. "—wishes."

If I didn't follow through with this, I'd always wonder. I looked at Grandma. I was sure she had figured that out about me. I had bolted up here first thing, unable to wait to find out what all of this was about.

"I'll try it for a while. But I can quit anytime I want, right?"

"Of course," She shot me a wry smile. "But you won't."

"Tuesday afternoons a good time for you?"

She nodded. "I'll make sure Heath gives you a ride."

"One more thing, Grandma Jewell. I researched what you told me and found an expert on line. I've been emailing him…"

Grandma Jewell feebly stood up and shouted. "No, no, absolutely not. Do not email or talk to anyone."

My mouth dropped open and Grandma Jewell continued, "I'm sorry child. I should have made it clearer. This is secret—just between us."

Shocked, I stuttered. "O…hh, sorry. I haven't really said much." I fibbed. "I'll write the guy back and tell him I made the whole thing up. He probably thinks I'm a nut anyway."

She calmed down. Worked for me, I didn't need to get involved with two "old" crazy people at the same time.

I left her room to find the others.

The day was enjoyable—more than nice. The gang consisted of all of the regulars with some additions—Constance (not too happy about that one), Patra, Iris, Bailey, Adrienne, Beth, a few football players, L.H., even Blue and Kate dropped by.

Heath was such a fierce competitor, I was glad I was on his team. We won easily and the cookout was scrumptious, the movie entertaining, and the ride home with Heath pleasant.

Heath stood at my front door. "I had a great time today."

"Me too." I meant it.

He leaned over and lightly kissed me on the cheek. "Good

night."

"Night." What a sweet kiss, I teared up as I went inside.

Mom, of course, was sitting there waiting up for me. "Did you have a good day?'

"The best." I skipped up the stairs.

I opened my journal. That was the first night I wrote more about Heath than I did about missing Z.

I was almost asleep. "Oh yeah, I'm supposed to write Mr. Lant back." I mumbled to myself and stumbled over to the laptop.

I sent off a quick email explaining I would not be able to meet with him, and I pretended that all that I'd written him had been false information fed to me by an unreliable source and that I was sorry I'd wasted his time.

I sent the email and immediately got an automatic reply.

Dear all,

We're sorry to report that Mr. Robert Lant was killed tonight. Specifics are sketchy, but it seems Mr. Lant was out for his nightly stroll with his eighteen-year-old constant companion, Bruiser his golden retriever, when he was shot by an alleged thief. The police have assured us that he died quickly and did not suffer. No suspects have been apprehended, but please keep his friends and family in your thoughts and prayers. His web page will provide updates and funeral arrangements.

With a heavy heart,

Jonathan Sullivan

Assistant, Mr. Robert Lant

Stunned, I whimpered. I hadn't really known him, but it was such a sad story. Then fear took over. My mind raced. Could this somehow be connected? The truck? The boat? The tattoo? It was too much to digest. I shook my head and scolded myself for trying to connect this trivial bizarre stuff that had been happening to me to a horrible murder. It couldn't possibly be connected. It didn't matter any way since there was nothing I could do about any of this, so I decided to put all of this out of my mind.

True to Grandma's word, the next Tuesday, Heath arrived at my house.

Heath was quiet on the ride.

After we drove into the garage, Heath said, "Let's just sit here a minute."

A few moments of uncomfortable silence followed. I finally glanced over at him. "What's going on?"

"I need to talk to you about something and I'm not sure how to approach it."

My mind went to all kinds of places. It sounded very serious. I finally breathed in heavily and gazed at him. "You can tell me anything. What is it?"

"I'm sorry, Leah."

"Sorry for what?" I was really curious now.

"This is uncomfortable." He stared at me and then averted his eyes. "Grandma told me about your talk with her the other day. That you said that you were worried I would get too physical too touchy feely. That I was trying to get serious too soon." He looked at me.

I froze, horrified. I had nothing to say. What was she up to?

He continued. "I just want you to know I'm not pushing anything."

My eyes got big and still I said nothing.

I zoned out. He ended with, "Don't feel like you have to tell my Grandma because you can tell me anything. Then are we okay?"

I nodded. He opened the door for me. As soon as I got out of the car, I ran to Grandma's room.

I knocked on the door and entered. "Grandma, did you tell Heath I thought he wanted our relationship to be something physical? And that I was upset with him?"

She patted the seat on the sofa next to her. "Of course I did, dear. You cannot have any of that adolescent physical hormone stuff. You have to focus on your lessons. We want to expand your gifts, right?"

I threw my backpack down and sat like a lump beside her. I

was furious.

She opened the handwritten book. "It seemed logical that if I told him, you wouldn't have to worry about him pawing on you anymore."

I fumed. "It wasn't like that."

"I know, dear. He's my grandson. He's a good boy. But good boys get carried away sometimes."

I realized I was relieved, but it still infuriated me. "Grandma Jewell, you don't run my life. I would appreciate it if you would mind your own business about my friends and friendships."

She nodded kind of half-heartedly. "We need to get started child."

What a meddler! She probably had been into everyone's business all of her life.

I calmed a bit. "It's okay, just don't let it happen again."

"We're going to try to expand your gifts an hour each week." She looked at me. "Now how old are you?"

"Fifteen." I squirmed. I had already answered that question once. Maybe Grandma did have a touch of dementia.

She clapped her hands together. "Perfect. Most abilities don't even start manifesting until the age of sixteen. That means you are going to have some powerful gifts if they started manifesting before the age of maturity. How exciting!"

I remembered this conversation from before, but I decided it wasn't worth the trouble to bring that fact up. "I guess." I glanced at the book.

She pulled out a clothespin. "We're going to work on one sense at the time. I need to get a starting point so we can measure how much you grow from week to week."

I pointed to the clothespin. "What's that for?"

She pulled out a blindfold and handed it to me. "You're going to close your nose shut and put this blindfold on. Then we're going to try a variety of foods and you're going to tell me what you think they are."

It seemed simple enough. I clasped the clothespin over my

nose and covered my eyes with the blindfold.

She tapped my shoulder. "When I tap your shoulder, open your mouth, and stick out your tongue."

I obliged. Something grainy was on my tongue. "Sugar?"

A clap. "Right!" This went on for a long time. She put strawberries, onions, carrots, ice cream, cookies of different flavors, potato chips, peanut butter, chocolate chips, orange juice, apples, and... well just about every food imaginable. I guessed them all correctly. Plus, I was full.

"Okay. How about this?"

I swished it around in my mouth. "I don't know."

She tapped her foot. "Make a guess anyway."

"For some reason, it reminds me of shoelaces."

She clapped her hands. "Take off the blindfold."

I spit out the stringy substance and there lying in my hand was a pair of wet shoelaces.

"Yuck! Why'd you give me shoelaces?" I spit some more.

She made some notes on a pad. "I wanted to see if you could tell me the taste of something you would never have ever tasted before."

She furrowed her eyebrows. "Your gifts could be more powerful than I realized."

"What now?"

She stood up. "Time to go home. That's all for today."

I grabbed my backpack and headed for the door. "See ya next Tuesday. Almost forgot to tell you, you don't have to worry about the man I was emailing."

"I wasn't worried." She waved, engrossed in her writings on the paper. "But why not?"

"He was murdered last night."

She gasped. "He was?"

I nodded.

Her skin paled and turned sallow. "Please be careful, dear."

I closed the door behind me.

Heath met me downstairs. "Have fun?" He chuckled and I

laughed with him and answered sarcastically. "*Sure*, loads of fun."

For the rest of February and all of March, I went over to Grandma's and had my lessons. Each week we tried a different sense. My answers were always accurate.

On a Tuesday late in March, I grabbed my backpack to leave as Grandma wrote furiously. I had no idea what she was writing, could have been about our sessions, she sure wasn't going to let me see it—no matter how hard I tried to peek.

"Grandma, we need to skip next week. Spring Break is coming up so I'll see you the following Tuesday."

She nodded half-paying attention and waved me out.

Heath was waiting for me as usual. "I have a surprise."

I climbed in the front seat of his car. "I love surprises."

He backed out of the driveway. "You'll have to wait till we get to your house."

All the way to my house, I tried to guess. I guessed a present, theme park trip, food, cake, something he made, something he'd written, and various other ridiculous things. Heath played along quite amused and savored telling me—"No"—each time.

We finally arrived at my house. He got out and walked in with me. My family, along with Kelly, Jane, Clay and all their families, were all sitting in my living room.

I couldn't imagine what this was all about. "What's going on?"

Heath started. "You know Spring Break is next week."

"Yeah?" I looked around the room. Everyone, but me, seemed to know the surprise.

"All of us," Heath motioned around the room. "Kelly, Jane, all the families are all going to —"

He stopped and took a deep breath. "—to Hawaii for Spring Break."

Chapter 21

I screamed. I was thrilled. I'd always wanted to go. Jane, Kelly, and I stood in a circle and jumped up and down. We squealed over and over again, "We're going to Hawaii. We're going to Hawaii."

I threw my arms around my dad's neck. "Thanks, Dad."

Dad swung me around and pointed to Heath. "Not my doing."

Kelly, Jane, and I almost knocked Heath down hugging him.

"We have three days to get ready so we better get cracking." Mom opened the door to let everyone out.

Hawaii was as beautiful as I had imagined. Locals met us with leis and played songs on the ukuleles to welcome us to the Big Island—very surreal. Caravans waited to carry us to Heath's family plantation.

The drive was a couple of hours, but well worth the trip. Palm trees lined the road as we turned into what looked like a five-star hotel.

Heath grabbed my waist and lifted me out of the van. "Welcome to my humble abode."

"Wow." I mumbled with my mouth wide open.

A team of maids and butlers gathered our bags.

Heath's dad motioned for us to follow. "We'll have a luau in about an hour. Everyone freshen up."

"O-M-G." Kelly exclaimed as she came into the room that was to be ours for the next seven days. "I've died and gone to heaven."

The room was as breathtakingly beautiful as the Hawaiian

scenery. It was the princess castle room that I had conjured up in my mind as a five-year-old child. Canopied beds draped by sheer fabrics, piled high with billowy pillows, were central to the bright and airy room. A pink and gold color palette covered the settees and lounge chairs so luxurious they would be fit for any queen. I half expected to see servants with large fans and platters of grapes wandering the room. It looked like a child's book illustration. Gorgeous!

The house overlooked a private beach that could be reached via our room's personal deck or by the communal one. All decks had a view of the bluff.

The first night we were treated to a traditional luau, the beach was overwhelmingly magnificent. Witnessing my first sunset in Hawaii, I noticed the sky was like none I had ever seen. I could have sworn that new colors had been made up just for Hawaii. The midnight blues with the hint of lavender paint brushed the sky as streaks of red-gold peeked out. No regular crayons colors allowed here. These shades should be in a box of their own.

Tables filled with a variety of foods—pineapple, ham, fruits of every kind, salads, too many items to eat—were ours for the taking at the buffet to end all buffets. We played limbo, ate, tried the hula, ate, and we laughed—a lot. Watching the tries at the hula dance proved not only entertaining, but also hilarious.

All the young people paired off. Terra played with the younger group, in an area off of Mom and Dad's bungalow.

"Look who I found—he's my age." Terra came running up with a boy who looked of Asian descent.

"Hello," I said. "And who are you?"

"Pan Otok." He smiled. "My brother Lee and the rest of our family missed the first plane. We had to come later."

The Otoks were here? Strange.

Then I recognized someone else.

Another familiar face.

Chapter 22

"Stone!" I ran up to him. "I didn't know you were coming."

He grinned. "Leah, these are my parents and my big sister, Chloe." Chloe looked like a porcelain doll. She had long silky hair and huge eyes. Besides Kate, I thought she was the prettiest girl I had ever seen.

Chloe playfully hit him on the shoulder. "I'm not big."

"And these are my little brothers, Kurt and Elijah, Eli for short, and my sister..." Stone pointed to his mom's pregnant belly. "Name to be announced later." We all chuckled.

I shook hands with the Poole family.

"Chloe's bunking with Kate and you girls in the *girl* bungalow." Heath's dad pointed toward our room and made the quote signs with his hands when he said "girl bungalow." I laughed. It looked odd for a grown man to do that. He grabbed a couple of bags and escorted the rest of the family to another area.

I walked up the path toward our room with Chloe. "I'll take you to meet the rest of the girls. Do you go to our school?"

"No, I'm at Berry Community College." She followed me up the trail.

"Oh."

Chloe dropped her stuff on the floor of our room and we started back.

I sat and watched as different people tried the hula. Locals tried to show each of us how to swing our hips. It got really hilarious when the men tried.

I studied the people, fascinated by the ages represented. Our young group ranged from not born yet to nineteen. Then there were the oldsters, the parents and grandparents. Because Mom had lost both her parents last year and Dad's parents were overseas, we hadn't brought our grandparents, but it seemed like everyone else had. The older group was especially comical trying to do the hula dance.

Toward the end of the night after a couple of people had retired to their bungalows, Heath's dad raised his goblet of wine. "Before everyone goes to bed, I'd like to propose a toast."

It took a couple of minutes to find and fill everyone's stemware. Everyone lifted his or her glasses. The younger crowd raised cups full of soda, milk, or juice.

Mr. Bolcan waited patiently. "I would like to thank all of my new and old friends for making this first annual gathering of...what shall we call it..." He paused and looked at some of the older grandmothers and grandfathers. "...we shall call it what I have called my paradise here on the island...our first gathering of the Island of the Star. May we enjoy getting to know each other, may we find our destiny, and may this be a glorious week for all of us."

Everyone drank. Grandma Jewell caught my eye and smiled a little. I remembered the significance of the Island of the Star. It was what the first five clans called their gathering place on the island of Alcatraz.

If it was a gathering then Z's family was missing. That night as I snuggled in my bed, I couldn't stop thinking about Z. After my bungalow mates fell asleep, I decided to walk around the enormous pineapple farm. I was sure it would be safe since it was a private plantation.

I walked out to the beach first and watched the waves break on the shore. It was so soothing that I burrowed in the sand and almost fell asleep when I heard talking.

Unsure of the voices' identities, I thought I better not reveal my presence. I crept up to a dune and listened. I recognized Grandma Jewell's voice and started to stand.

A male voice I didn't recognize answered her. "That Kate girl is going to be a problem."

I knelt back down and crept in a little closer. What problem could Blue's girlfriend Kate cause?

A female said, "I think the presence of Chloe will change that. Chloe is Blue's destiny. He must be the chosen one. He has to be. He is the first born of the Sky."

Another male interjected, "I'm not sure. I have seen no signs of it. I think my grandson Stone should not be underestimated."

The voices grew louder and more garbled. I heard mentions such as "....my grandson, Lee...Heath was an obvious choice..."

Grandma Jewell broke in. "Quit arguing. We do not choose these things. We can only interpret."

The voices calmed.

Someone asked, "Grandma Jewell, you have studied the book and made more notations than any of us. Do you think this is the time of the prophecy?"

I strained to hear. Was she going to tell them about me? I closed my eyes and waited to be sold down the river. I heard Grandma answer. "I haven't seen any signs yet, but I will keep my eyes open."

I breathed a sigh of relief.

Another male said, "We need to strengthen our clans through marriage."

I heard murmurs of agreement. "Many of our daughters should be in line to claim the elder sons, Blue, Heath, Stone, and Lee."

"Don't forget Neb." A voice answered, "The eldest and strongest."

Grandma asked again, "Which daughters exactly?'

The same voice answered, "I've done the family trees. All the daughters should be given high marks except one."

"Who?" Grandma asked.

The voice once again answered. "Leah. She should be promised last. She and Jorden split in their genes. They are splits and not true wholes. They are halves of one. They'll not produce great offspring."

I burned with anger.

Another voice asked, "Why would you think that?"

"In all of our clans there have never been great ones that were twins. Isn't that true, Grandma Jewell?"

I assumed Grandma Jewell agreed or at least didn't oppose because the male voice continued. "I propose that we make sure that Leah and Jorden are not promised to any first born."

Another male interrupted. "If Leah is not promised to Heath, I claim her as wife for one of my brother's boys."

I sat back and took a deep breath. This was my premonition.

I knew I was too young to get married, but just the thought of someone trying to set up my future... my whole life. The gall. I controlled my life. I'd ignore what I'd heard. What planet did these crazy old folks live on? They were freaking nuts if they thought—

Then I heard "it." *The Voice.* "Leah will make her own choice."

Hearing T*he Voice* chilled my soul. Nevertheless, one thing was for certain; T*he Voice* was right.

Chapter 23

I tried to get a glimpse of the speaker. I peeked up and heard something that made me hide again.

"Was the problem with the Starre family and that girl Leah straightened out?"

The Starre family? Z? I strained to listen. "Yes, we had them—"

"Missy." A voice behind me startled me. I looked up at the face of one of the maids who had helped me earlier with my bag.

I scrunched down, grabbed the house cleaner, and pulled her down beside me in the sand.

"Sshh!" I whispered.

One of the voices said, "What's that noise?"

"It's probably time to go anyway. We'll meet again in the morning."

Then silence.

I sat with the maid beside me, my hand clamped over her mouth.

After I heard everyone shuffle off, I took my hand away. "Sorry."

She stood and pulled me up. "You okay, Missy?"

"Yeah, you just scared me." I walked back with her down the trail. She seemed to not need a big explanation. I wasn't really sure if she understood anything I said.

I walked into my room and waved goodbye to her. I collapsed on my bed with lots to think about. It seemed to me the clans, or at least the older generation, knew about each other. I couldn't decide if that was good or bad. I thought about my own great grandparents. Where were they from? I could remember my mother and father trying to give me information about my ancestors and how I had blown them off.

I remembered saying, "I don't have to know about them. They're all dead."

How callous I must have sounded! I was probably about nine or ten the last time they had tried to tell me about my great-grandparents. I concentrated. I remembered my mother's mother and father were from Alabama. We saw them from time to time. I wished now I could see them again.

Wait! It wasn't my mother's parents who would be a part of the clan. She married into the clan. If I believed Grandma Jewell, we were the missing point of the five point star. My dad would have been a direct descendant of the Sky Clan. He would have been born from the only survivor.

I thought of the book, *Last of the Mohicans*. I guess my dad's people were the last of the Sky Clan. No, because me, Blue, Jorden and Terra were here. Crazy thinking! My head was just too full. Sometimes when you think too hard and too long your body just gives up; I fell asleep from pure exhaustion.

"Leah."

I rolled over and saw Heath standing beside my bed.

I glanced at the clock. "What time is it?"

"A little after three," he said.

"Three in the morning?" I sat up and rubbed the sleep out of my eyes.

He laughed. "No, three in the afternoon. You slept most of the day away. Are you going to get up?"

He couldn't know about my escapade the previous night so I made up an excuse. "Must have jet lag. Be out in a minute. I'm starving."

"I'll bet you are. We're at the beach. See you in a minute." He walked out.

I got up, took a quick shower, and put on my pink bathing suit and the eyelet sundress. As I walked out, the delicious smell of food overpowered me.

I walked the trail and caught up with the couples Kelly and Jorden, Clay and Jane, and Blue and Kate sitting together and looking all lovey-dovey. Heath, Chloe, Stone, Adrienne, Lee, and Astrid seemed to be involved in an intense conversation.

I stood by Heath. "Where's the food?"

"Behind you." He pointed over to a bunch of tables with a feast spread on top of them. My senses were supposed to be so strong. *How'd I miss that?*

I made my way to the food table. It smelled delicious. I scanned the area to see if I saw any of the grandmas or grandfathers, but to no avail. They were nowhere to be seen.

I filled a plate with strawberries, crepes, ham, a banana soufflé, and some croissants, and then sat by Heath. "Where's everybody else?'

Adrienne grabbed a strawberry off my plate. "We're all here."

"No, I mean the older people. " I guarded my plate with my hand. "Where are they?"

Heath grabbed another strawberry from under my hand. I moved my plate away from him. "Get your own plate. There's plenty."

He smirked. "But that's no fun. I saw Grandma this morning. I think they had some sort of tour for them. I don't know where."

I was disappointed. I had planned to go around to every one of them, introduce myself, and see if I could recognize *The Voice*. It was my mission for the day.

I handed Heath a strawberry. I wasn't above a bribe. "So when are they coming back?"

He bit into it. "I don't know. Want me to check?"

Lee leaned in. "Hey, did you hear about Neb and Z and Stella?"

I swallowed hard and tried to act nonchalant. "No, what about them?" The old people search left my mind.

Lee leaned back on his hands. "Neb and Stella might be coming back to school. I think their father is finished with whatever he was doing in Alaska."

Won't someone please ask the question I was burning to know? No one did. It was up to me. "What about Z?"

Lee stood up. "Oh Z, I heard that he had fallen for some girl in Alaska and they couldn't get him to come back."

I dropped my plate, spilling my food onto the sand.

"Sorry." I picked up the sand-covered cuisine and scooped it back onto the plate trying to hide the intense pain in my gut. I hurt to the core and just when I thought it couldn't get any worse. It did.

Lee jumped and ran calling back over his shoulder. "Hey guys, I'm going to the beach." He stopped mid-run and shot a thumbs-up sign back at me. "Good thing you've got Heath now or you'd be dumped for some Eskimo girl."

Everyone leapt up and took off. I couldn't move.

Chapter 24

Kelly immediately came back to me. "You okay?"

The tears came. "I gotta get out of here I don't want the rest to see." I turned my back to her.

Kelly was truly a good friend. She yelled down to the others. "Think that Leah ate too fast. She's sick. I'm going to take her back up to the bungalow. She probably just needs to get rid of the food she just wolfed down."

Heath started back. Kelly held up her hand. "Nobody wants their boyfriend to see them puking."

The boyfriend comment must have worked because I caught a glimpse of Heath's smiling face before he went back to the beach.

"Thanks." I looked at Kelly through tear-blurred eyes.

She put her hand on my shoulder. "You wanta talk about it?"

"Probably should. " I walked toward the trail. "Might make me feel better."

We walked in silence. I finally sat down on a bench and Kelly sat by me. "I really thought he'd come back."

"I know you never talked about it, but I could tell you really cared about him." She took a deep breath. "I think Jorden really cared about Stella too."

I had never thought about what Stella coming back could mean to Kelly. Would Jorden drop Kelly and go back to Stella? I really don't think so.

I patted her reassuringly. "I think Jorden really cares about you too, Kelly."

"I know he does." She smiled. "My point is that sometimes relationships just aren't meant to be. Like I think Stella and Jorden weren't meant to be, and that Jorden and I—maybe we're supposed to be."

I smiled weakly. I knew where she was going with this.

She leaned over to me. "Maybe you ought to give Heath a chance. It sounds as if Z has moved on. Maybe it's time you did too."

I dropped my arms from around her. She knew me better than I thought.

She squeezed me harder. "Really give Heath a chance—not just going through the motions."

I cried softly in her arms. Maybe she was right and I should open up to Heath. I hadn't really. In this beautiful, gorgeous land, I could really look at Heath with my whole heart and see if I could let him in. I would try anything to get rid of this pain.

We went back to the others at the beach.

Heath ran to me as soon as he saw us. I darted up to him and hugged him hard. He pulled me back.

I think he was surprised at my show of emotion. "You all right?"

"Yeah." I needed someone. I would hang onto Heath. If Z could move on, then maybe I could too.

That night we had another luau, but my heart wasn't in it. Determined to put on a fake happy face, I tried to let everyone know that Heath and I were a couple now. I followed him around like a puppy dog. I just wanted to shut people like Lee up.

At the end of the night, Heath walked me back to my bungalow. I pulled him away from the path and headed down to a secluded area. I knew what I wanted—revenge on Z. I put my arms around Heath's neck and leaned up to kiss him.

He grabbed my arms and pushed me away. "Not like this, Leah. I don't want an angry kiss. I want something more. I thought we—"

Enraged, I spat my words at him, "Maybe I'm not good enough for you. Maybe I'm not good enough for anybody. Maybe it's me."

136

Crying, I turned my back to him.

"Leah, a broken heart takes time—" he began.

I didn't want to hear it. I darted off. He ran after me. I hid in the bushes until he jogged past. I was horrified. *Everyone knew how I felt about Z.* I walked and walked. I sat down in the grass and sobbed uncontrollably. I don't know how long I sat there, but the sky rumbled and rain spilled forth from the sky with fury. I sprinted down the trail and then veered off onto a grassy area, this time trying to escape the rain. I stopped when I realized I was lost.

Nothing looked familiar. I searched my pockets for my phone. I hadn't taken it. I had no way to communicate with anyone. No one knew where I was. It was dark now. The kind of dark that happens when there are no street or house lights. Spooky dark. Scary dark.

Frightened, I wondered how I was going to get back. "*Think*, I told myself." I listened for the waves breaking to find the beach, but the storm muffled all other sounds.

I thought of my gifts Grandma Jewell and I had been working on. I should be able to find my way. I needed to listen, to see, and to smell. The rain pelted down. The sky looked as upset as I was and the downpour bombarded me.

I sat in a yoga position and put everything out of my mind. I transcended the rain and the thunder and lightning. I concentrated on finding a sound or smell that I would recognize and I finally heard it.

I listened. It wasn't *The Voice*. It was faint. I closed my eyes. I blocked out all sound. It wasn't beach waves.

A voice.

A familiar voice.

It was Jorden.

Chapter 25

It was faint at first, but I concentrated. *"Blue and I are in trouble. We need your help."*

I followed Jorden's voice. He said the same words over and over.

I walked through the storm determined to find my way back. I didn't realize how far I had run until I came upon the trail. I made my way back to the plantation as dawn was breaking.

Jorden never stopped calling. His plea grew stronger and louder. I followed his voice. Then I saw her.

My mother sat outside the bungalow crying. She jumped up when she saw me. "Something happened."

"I know." I walked past her to a silent form lying unmoving in a bed. I knew who it was. Jorden was hooked to machines surrounded by a couple of nurses and what looked to be a doctor.

I sat down by my ashen-faced twin. "I'm here." I whispered in his ear.

He was unconscious, but I heard him talking to me in my mind. *"You have to pull me out of this."*

"I know." I said out loud. I knew what to do. I sat by Jorden and I concentrated on him. I placed my hands on him. I rested my head beside his.

"It's working." I heard his voice inside my head.

I closed my eyes.

"Leah." Jorden put his hand on my head. "I'm okay now."

I looked at Jorden and realized he was talking out loud. I

hugged him. The doctor and nurses made notes and fiddled with the machines, but didn't attempt to move me.

He grimaced in pain. "Leah, where've you been?"

I touched his face as his color was coming back. "Everywhere, except where I should have been. What happened?"

"Blue and I were in a wreck."

I felt a pang of fear. "Where's Blue?"

"Leah." He pulled me close and whispered in my ear. "Somehow I knew there was danger and to grab Blue and jump out of the car. How did I know?" He started crying. "Is Blue all right?"

I told him the truth. "I don't know. I'll go find out."

I crawled out of his bed and went to the door. I saw Mom. "Where's Blue?"

Mom grabbed me and hugged me. "We were worried sick about you. We looked everywhere. No one could find you."

"I wandered off and got lost. Sorry, Mom." I pulled away. "Is Blue all right?"

She cried. "The car Blue and Jorden were in was hit by a truck and burst into flames. The car driver was killed and witnesses saw the truck driver jump out and run off."

"Grace, is Blue okay? Jorden wants to know?"

Mom seemed disoriented. "Jorden's awake and talking?" She rushed into Jorden's room.

Kelly ran up to me. "Did you say Jorden's awake?"

I nodded to her. She ran to be by Jorden's side. No use trying to get anything out of them. I looked for Kate. I knew Kate would be with Blue. I opened a door and found them both—Blue lying on the bed not moving and Kate sitting by his side stroking his hair.

I walked in. "Is he going to be okay?"

She nodded.

Blue opened his eyes. He was bruised badly. His face was swollen and his arm was in a sling. "Hey, where were you? Heath came and said you had run off. We got one of the plantation workers to take us around and look for you."

I felt sick. Someone was dead and it was my fault.

Everything went black.

Chapter 26

"Leah." My mother called.

I opened my eyes. I was on a bed.

"Leah." She pulled my shirt off and wrapped me in a blanket. "You fainted and you're soaking wet from the rain. We need to get the rest of these wet clothes off you."

I helped my mother pull off my jeans. She swaddled me in the blanket. I felt warmer.

It took me a minute to get my bearings. Where was I? Oh yeah, in Hawaii.

I stared at my mother, only one thought on my mind. "Did that driver die because of me?"

My mother put a warm towel on my head. "What are you talking about?"

I cried the words. "The driver."

"I don't understand?"

I held my hand to my chest trying to hold my emotion in. "They were trying to find me. Blue and Jorden. They were looking for me and now the driver is dead."

"Leah, Blue and Jorden were riding with the driver to get supplies. Heath called them about your disappearance. They hadn't had a chance to start looking for you when the truck hit them." She touched the damp towel. "So no, it wasn't your fault."

I breathed a sigh of relief. I couldn't stand having someone's death on me. I sat up. "What happened?'

"It's almost like the truck driver intentionally tried to push them into that gas truck." She removed the towel.

"Intentionally?" I repeated. "Who knew Blue and Jorden were in the car?"

My mother wrung out the towel over a basin. "I guess everyone. They left when we were all gathering for dinner. Why?"

"No reason." What if someone was trying out to wipe out my Skye family just as they had tried to centuries ago? I thought of Mr. Lant's emails. Could Mr. Lant have been murdered because of all of this? What was going on? A shiver went down my spine.

Crazy thinking—but was it any more crazy than going to "gift lessons" with an old lady who believed that ancestors of five clans were destined to reunite? And who believed I was a special person sent here to reunite five clans and discussed arranged marriages like it was normal. I couldn't think anymore.

"I'm tired." I said to my mother.

She said what all good mothers say: "Sleep now baby. We'll think about this in the morning."

I decided to take her advice. I fell asleep. My body was about to give in anyway.

I opened my eyes. My mother was asleep with her head in my lap. I moved and she roused awake. "Good morning girlie-girl."

She looked tired.

"How long have I been asleep?" My eyes came into focus and I spotted Heath sitting asleep in a chair.

"About two days." She pointed to Heath. "He hasn't left the room."

She sat on the side of my bed and whispered to me. "Look Leah, Heath told us that you two had a fight and that is why you ran off. Leah you're too young to be so serious. You've got your whole life in front of you. Slow down."

She pointed at him as he started to stir. "He seems like a nice boy, but all this boyfriend and girlfriend drama—" She kissed my forehead. "—you've got plenty of time for that later on— okay little girl?"

142

I nodded. I hated it when she got in my business.

She left the room and Heath came over. "Leah, I'm sorry."

I grabbed his hand. "You've got nothing to be sorry about. I'm sorry for being such an immature brat. I don't know why you don't leave me too."

He squeezed my hand. "Leah, I'm your friend and I'll always be here for you."

I looked up at him. "I know that and I will always be your friend too."

I couldn't help, but love him on some level.

The Skye family left before anyone else from our Hawaiian paradise. We had to. Blue was bruised up. Jorden had barely survived the wreck; I had scarcely survived the storm. Mom and Dad were exhausted. I felt sorry for Terra, but if I was honest, I'd be glad when Spring Break ended.

Kate, Jane, Clay, and Kelly's family came back with us. I spent the rest of Spring break recuperating. Jorden and Blue made miraculous recoveries.

I decided to not think about the prophecy, the wreck, or Z. Especially not about Z being with another girl. I was glad when I saw that the renters were still there. I couldn't bear to see Neb and Stella. I didn't want my face rubbed in it. I was furious at Z. I hated him and was glad he was in Alaska.

At the end of the week I received an email from Mr. Lant's assistant requesting my address. It said Mr. Robert Lant had left me something. Heeding Grandma Jewell's warnings, I decided to ignore it.

On Monday, I was a little apprehensive about going to school since I wasn't sure how much everyone knew about the drama in Hawaii. I decided to pretend nothing had happened. That seemed to work just fine.

Constance, Patra, and the rest of their group probably would have given me a hard time except they were to angry at not being invited to Hawaii. The last thing I needed was the mean girls razzing me even more.

Kelly announced at lunch, "Berry's having a gala. They're not calling it a prom. Seems we are too good for a prom. We have to have a *gala*." She air-quoted "gala."

I laughed. "Really?"

"Yeah. We're supposed to get all dressed up for it in fancy clothes. There'll be a band." She shrugged her shoulders in "duh" fashion. "That's a prom, right?"

I nodded. "I guess."

Jorden grabbed Kelly's hand. "If it looks like a prom and it acts like a prom, then it must be a prom." Jorden got down on one knee in the lunchroom "Kelly will you be my date for the..." He cleared his throat. "...the gala."

Kelly laughed. "Of course. Who are you going with, Leah?"

Heath overheard us. "With me I hope, her boyfriend-in-waiting. Oh by the way, the gala is having a sit-down dinner, I don't think a prom has that."

He went down on one knee too. "Leah, will you do me the honor of letting me escort you to the gala?"

Constance rolled her eyes in disgust. She really hates me and this isn't going to help.

I answered, "I guess so. Since you are my B-I-W."

He cocked one eyebrow.

"You know B-I-W, boyfriend-in-waiting."

He laughed. "Grandma Jewell wants to know if you're coming back this Tuesday."

I honestly hadn't thought about it. "Not this week. Maybe next Tuesday. I need a little break."

He smiled. "I'll tell her. I think she missed you."

Early Saturday morning Kelly's mom, my mom, Kelly, Jane, and I trekked over to Central Lake Mall. Mom insisted, "A little retail therapy never hurt anyone." The plan was to buy gala dresses, eat lunch, see an afternoon movie, and drive home. A girls' day out was just what we all needed. It had been far too long.

It ended up being a flawless outing where everything you try on fits perfectly and was reasonably priced. Kelly settled on a royal blue spaghetti strapped, tea length number and Jane decided on a dreamy yellow stretch long dress with a slit that accentuated her long legs. I picked out a red strapless dress that I fell in love with; mom fell in love with the price. Red was definitely my color.

The only negative of the day was the mean girl clique. All girls love the mall. Even mean girls.

Constance waited until the Moms were out of the room before she pounced. She sneered at Kelly. "You look like a boy in a girl's dress." The others in her group giggled as she continued. "Leah, you look like a lobster and Jane who told you yellow was your color. C'mon girls, we don't want this scraggly group to rub off on us. They're pathetic. I almost feel sorry for them." She shot a look at me. "Almost." And with that, they walked off.

I hated her. I wished my mom could hear how mean Constance was, but Constance knew exactly how to turn on the charm around Moms; they loved her.

We ate lunch in the center of the mall so everyone could have her pick of cuisine. The movie we chose had just the right amount of comedy and romance. The mean girls tried, but they weren't able to ruin the nice day.

As we left, I headed to the bathroom planning to meet the rest at the entrance to the mall.

Just as I was about to reach the front of the mall I saw her.

Stella.

What was Stella doing here?

Chapter 27

I picked up my steps.

Constance caught me. "Lost? You are one dumb southern girl." What was she talking about? She stood blocking me and by the time I got away, Stella was gone. Could I have been imagining it?

I got a call from Kelly. "Where are you?"

I headed out to meet up with my group. I must have been seeing things, it couldn't possibly have been Stella.

The next few weeks in biology we learned about dissection. Instead of visiting The Florida State University Medical School, the doctors from Tallahassee lectured our class. I would have enjoyed the field trip, but with all that had happened I was happy that the trip had not worked out and we would be staying on campus. The lectures were great; I loved every minute of it.

Mr. Bolcan was so rich, he bought us life-like plastic cadavers. We were going to get to perform autopsies on these pseudo humans. Reading about it in books was one thing, but making actual cuts and stitches was quite another. During the first week of the autopsy session, we'd see an autopsied cadaver, and then our teacher would perform the autopsy on an uncut plastic cadaver. In the final weeks, we would perform a step-by-step autopsy in student groups on an uncut body. I was thrilled. I couldn't wait.

On Tuesday morning, Heath met me before class. "I'll pick you up here right after school."

I wrinkled my brow. "What for?"

He tapped my forehead with the eraser of a pencil. "Did you forget Grandma?"

I had. "I'll be there. See you at lunch."

I was happy to be seeing Grandma today. Maybe she could shed some light on the set-up marriage conversation I'd overheard in Hawaii or tell me how I had known what Jorden was saying when he was unconscious or if Blue's car accident had anything to do with all of the clan stuff. But most of all, maybe she could tell me who *The Voice* was.

"Grandma." I walked into her room. "I'm here."

She wasn't there. I dropped my backpack to wait on her. I pulled out the handwritten book from under the table and started flipping through it.

I scanned through the pages I'd seen, the prophecy, the clans, and the rules. I turned to a page about gifts and found mine. It was entitled, "Heightened Senses."

I found a folded page. I opened it up. It read: "Map of Fountain of the Island of the Star." It was in a language I couldn't read. Grandma must have deciphered it, as there were a couple of pieces of notebook paper with symbols and words slipped in among the pages. One had a list of symbols with the words: fountain, youth, rebirth of soul, map. Wouldn't it be awesome if this had something to do with Ponce de Leon and his search for The Fountain of Youth?

The map was crude, but I identified California and Alcatraz. A trail was marked from California to North Texas to North Carolina to Alabama to a place close to Berry.

"Leah." Grandma startled me and I slammed the book shut. "What are you doing?"

"Oh, hi." I straightened my skirt. "Just looking at the book. What's the map all about?"

"It's a legend." She sat on the sofa. "Sorry I was late. I got caught up with the gardener. I was helping him plant some annuals and lost track of time."

"That's all right." I gestured to the door. "It was open so I just let myself in. Hope that was okay."

"It's fine, dear." She seized the book. "But I need to show you this little by little so you understand it."

"Is the map showing The Fountain of Youth?" I tried to open the book, but she held it closed.

"See, that's what I'm talking about." She patted my hand. "All in good time, dear, all in good time."

I shrugged and pulled my list of questions out of my pocket.

She eyed the paper. "You have a list?"

I pursed my lips and scrunched up my face. "I have a lot of questions. Hawaii was wonderful, but also scary and confusing."

She sat, pensive for a moment. "I'll try to answer."

I surveyed my list. Scrawled on my paper were *set-up marriages, talking to Jorden, Blue's accident, Z, voice.*

"First, arranged marriages." I glanced up at her. "That's not something the clan practices nowadays. Right?"

"Of course not, dear." She folded her hands and cocked her head. "Where did you hear that?'

I lied. "I didn't hear it. I just thought with all the rules and stuff. So that's not practiced at all. People can marry whomever they want or be with whomever they want or not marry if they want. There is no pressure from the *clan*." I said clan with imaginary quotes.

"Do you want to get married?" She caught me off guard.

"Of course not." I decided to move on. "Next question. When Jorden was unconscious in Hawaii, I heard him talking in my head. How is that possible?"

She thought. "You're a twin—that happens sometimes with twins. Or maybe you are hearing his Second Voice."

I interrupted. "Second Voice? What's that?"

She continued. "You've heard of second sight—when people think they're psychic. Second Voice is where you hear what's going to be said or what wants to be said."

"What do you mean?" I looked at her. "What's going to be said?"

She put her hands to her throat. "Our brain sends the message

148

to our larynx and we say what we tell ourselves to say. If we can't talk, like your brother, then our mind keeps sending the message; but our body just can't follow through. Some people are thought to be able to hear that second voice. What wants to be said, but cannot be said. Our brain edits what we say."

I interrupted again, "Like think before you speak."

She grinned. "Yes, we catch ourselves when we think about saying something about the girl who has gained too much weight or a horrible haircut. We think it, we communicate it and we do all that we need to do in order to say it...we just don't say it."

"Interesting, could hearing a second voice make someone think they were hearing voices?"

Grandma nodded. "I suppose it could."

Possibly the answer to the voices I'd been hearing, but I wouldn't share that just yet. "I'll give that one some more thought. " I looked at my list. "Moving on, Blue's accident. Any thoughts on that? Could it have been on purpose?"

She patted my leg. "I heard what the reports said. Not sure if it was on purpose. By the way, how are Blue and Jorden?"

I studied her. She seemed genuinely concerned. "They're healing quickly. It's amazing. Almost back to normal."

She nodded. "Good. Any more questions?"

I pushed my finger down the list. "Two more. Do you know anything about the Starre family from Alaska?"

"No." She answered too quickly and looked too uncomfortable to be telling the truth.

I didn't know how to pursue the topic further so I moved on. "I heard *The Voice* that's in my head again."

"You did." Her eyes lit up. "I thought you understood that might be a second voice."

"No, I don't think it's the second voice. I don't think you understand. In Hawaii, I *actually* heard who has been talking to me." I watched for her reaction.

I said, "Actually *The Voice*. I heard *The Voice* in Hawaii."

She seemed afraid. "That can't be. Do you know who was

149

talking?"

I continued, "No. That's why I'm asking you."

"I'm glad your brothers are healing." Grandma Jewell breathed a sigh of relief. "Any more questions?"

"I guess not."

How frustrating! She wasn't going to give me any information unless it was on her time schedule. I had to find a way around that.

Chapter 28

After finishing my homework that night, I went into the kitchen to help with supper. "What're we having Mom?"

She pulled out a pound of bacon and put a pan on the stove. "BLTs and chips. How does that sound?"

"Yummy." I opened the refrigerator to get out some lettuce and tomatoes to slice. "Hey, I know your people are from Alabama. Where are Dad's people from?"

She stood over the pan as the bacon sizzled. "I remember your grandmother once telling of your great-great-great—I don't know how many greats— grandparents from a long way off moving from California to Texas. They settled somewhere in north Texas near Abilene, I think."

I arranged the cut tomatoes on a plate. "Where to after that?"

She plucked the crisp bacon, placed it on a paper-toweled plate, and put more in the skillet. "I think some people moved from Texas to...?"

I added, "North Carolina?"

"Yeah." She looked at me. "How'd you know that?"

"Musta heard Dad talk about it."

She smiled. "I know how you knew that." She pointed at my neck. "— from your ruby."

I glanced down. "My ruby?"

"The ruby came from the North Carolina mines. Remember? You got it from your grandmother." She waved the spatula in the air. "It's been passed down."

"Yeah. So how'd our people get to Berry?"

She removed the last cooked bacon slices and carried the heaping platter to the dining room table. "I don't guess your dad's told you the story of your great-great-grandfather." I shook my head and she continued, "We have a few minutes. Sit and I'll tell you."

"The Skye family who migrated to North Carolina believed in a curse that they felt had followed their lineage. They decided to keep moving, hoping a great treasure would be revealed."

"Great treasure?'

She waved her hand. "Not treasures like gold, but a treasure of information. The myth told of a person born from the Skye lineage who would bring together the clans. They traveled from North Carolina to Alabama. There they met a former prisoner of Alcatraz, the prison off the coast of California."

A familiar tone to this story.

She continued, "This prisoner claimed to have found a map that contained the path to The Fountain of Youth, the one that Ponce de León was looking for in Florida."

Mom took a quick sip of sweet tea. "This man claimed that The Fountain of Youth was magical for the chosen one."

She chuckled and waved her hand dismissively. "It's a lot of hocus pocus. He told me that story while I was at the University of Alabama finishing my nursing degree. It was so whimsical. I thought he was the most interesting man I'd ever met."

Her face went all soft, dreamy, and mushy gushy. "It was that story that led to us falling in love and getting married. After graduation, we moved to be closer to Gamma, Dad's grandmother. We got jobs in Berry and we've been here ever since. My parents visited with Gamma on the day she died when I was pregnant with you and Jorden. We all like listening to the old stories. Gamma told some humdingers."

"What kind of hocus pocus?"

She shook her head and giggled. "Who knows? I think hearing voices."

I coughed.

She hit me on the back. "You okay?"

I coughed a little more. "In biology today, we got to see the first plastic cadaver, very cool."

Mom looked confused over the subject change. "G...great. I guess."

I kept nattering. "We named the cadavers. One, we named Oberon, probably because we are studying *A Midsummer's Night Dream* in English."

I took a breath. "Some might name their cadavers Puck or Titania."

I kept chattering, trying not to think about the strange coincidences and how uncomfortable I felt. I'd ask Grandma Jewell about that fountain next Tuesday.

Mom would interject the obligatory uh-huh every once in awhile as I spoke trivial nonsense. "I think we are going to name ours Brad the Bod and Lee who is obsessed with *A Streetcar Named Desire* is naming his cadaver Stanley or Stella."

Mom interrupted, "Speaking of Stella, guess what I heard about the Starre family?"

"What?"

She placed square brick red plates on the flowery placemats beside the folded the napkins. "I heard they may come back next year. I think Neb got accepted to Florida State."

"Have you heard anything else about Stella or anything about ...Z?" I tried to sound as uninterested as I could.

Her eyes widened and she tapped her chin. "Probably just gossip, but I heard it and I was afraid you might. I'd rather you heard it from me."

She took a big breath. "I hate to tell you this, but I heard he was engaged to a tribal princess from Alaska and because she is pregnant they have to get married soon."

I sunk in the chair with a thump.

She asked, "He's old news, right?"

I stuffed back my emotions. "I want him to be happy. Nothing physical ever happened between us."

153

Mom breathed in a sigh of relief. "You're too young for that anyway."

I burned with anger, anger at my mom for not understanding and at myself for what I was feeling, but most of all anger at Z for leaving me with no explanation.

Completely defeated, my shoulders slumped. The energy drained from my face.

Mom's eyes softened. She had the look of pity I'd seen on her face the last time she visited her dad before he died. "First loves are always hard."

Defiantly, I announced. "I'm focusing all of my energy on becoming the best doctor I can be. Maybe the greatest doctor of all time. I won't have time for boys until much later or maybe never."

"It's your choice, Leah." She rested her hand on mine. "Don't let anyone ever tell you different."

I couldn't stand to think of Z with someone else. It physically made me sick. But I couldn't tell my mom about that. All of our times together flooded my mind. Did he ever give me a hint there was someone else? Never! I would never understand. Ever!

As usual, Mom could see my turmoil. "Leah, go out and have fun. Date different boys, see if you like any of them."

"Grace, stay out of my business. I'll figure out my life all for myself without your help. How many times do I have to tell you things are different now that they were in the olden days? You're always meddling."

I hurt to my core and I felt a twinge of guilt for spewing that pain and hate out at my mother. What I was feeling had nothing to do with her.

Chapter 29

"**G**low's is having teen night on Friday," Clay announced at our lunch table.

Kelly slipped into her usual seat beside Jorden. "Isn't that a bar?"

"I guess, but—" Clay pulled out a flyer. "Friday night's for sixteen to twenty. No drinking."

I tapped him on the shoulder. "Uh...hello...me, Kelly, and Jane are only fifteen."

Jane held up her hand. "Speak for yourself. I turn sixteen May 2nd."

I shook my finger. "You're *still* not sixteen."

"I think it'll be okay," Clay said. "They mostly I.D. for being too old. I don't think they'll I.D. you. We'll just leave if you can't get in. Everybody's going."

Heath put his arm around my shoulder. "It could be fun."

Kelly and Jane pleaded.

I couldn't refuse. "Why not?"

Besides, I needed a night out.

Jane and I went to Kelly's to get ready. I picked out jean shorts and a revealing crop top. I curled my hair and put on more makeup than usual.

Clay was correct. They never gave us a second glance. We ordered some "virgin" Piña Coladas and non-alcoholic beers.

They had a karaoke machine. The longer the night went on,

the braver people got, first dancing, and then singing. Constance, Patra, Beth, and Iris sang *Short People,* but substituted the word "your" for "short" and pointed to me, Kelly, and Jane when they sang. What was it about us that they hated so much and what was it about them that we disliked so much? My group sang an old Supremes song, *Stop in the Name of Love.*

The boys decided to play pool instead of singing.

Constance sashayed by and said so we could overhear. "Those girls are nothing but trash."

Wish she'd leave us alone!

A server came up with three new "virgin" Piña Coladas. "Compliments of the table over there."

Three older-looking boys waved at us. One had a full beard, the other had both arms tattooed, and the third had piercings on his lips and eyebrows.

"Who are they?" I asked Jane and Kelly and they didn't know.

Kelly asked, "Should we accept? "

I whispered, "What do you think, Jane?"

"They look too old, maybe we overdid the looking older thing, besides—" Jane motioned toward Clay at the pool table. "—I don't want *him* to get mad."

Kelly nodded. "I don't want Jorden mad either."

Kelly grabbed the server as she was delivering the drinks. "Could you take them back? We have dates."

I helped the server put the drinks back on the tray. "Be nice to them, but tell them thanks, but no thanks."

We watched her as she took the untouched drinks back over to them. They stood up immediately and headed over to our table.

Kelly shook her head. "They're coming over. I don't want any trouble. Maybe they think we're alone."

I stood. "I gotta pee anyway. You two go back over with our guys. I'll be over there in a minute.

Kelly and Jane nodded.

I grabbed my purse. "I won't be long."

When I came out of the bathroom, the bearded guy grabbed

me. "I think we ought to party, baby." He smelled of liquor.

I pushed him away. "Look, I'm here with someone." I noticed a familiar star tattoo inside his wrist.

He grabbed my upper arm, and squeezed pulling me closer to him.

My ribs were crushed as I struggled to free myself. "Leave me alone. I mean it."

He held me where I couldn't move. I attempted to turn around to spot my group.

"Don't worry about your friends." He glanced back over his shoulder. "We have Sissy and May Belle taking care of them. They'll be busy for a while."

I caught a glimpse of two girls with Jorden and Clay. Clay, Jorden, Kelly, and Jane seemed to be arguing with two girls. Heath looked like he was refereeing the fray. I couldn't get their attention. "You're hurting me."

He rubbed the tip of his finger down my arm. "We don't want to hurt you." His voice creeped me out. "We just want to get to know you a little better."

The other two boys laughed out loud. "A lot better." I could smell alcohol on all them.

I pulled away and yelled. "Leave me alone!"

My outburst got some attention. A bouncer came over. "You have to leave. You're drunk and I'm certain you are over the age limit. Take your girl with you. This is kiddie night. You're not allowed in here."

"I'm not…" The guy clamped his hand on my cheeks and pressed them together. "Babe, don't talk back to the man. We don't want no trouble. We'll leave. Sorry. My girl just makes me crazy." He forced me to move, one hand held tightly onto my cheeks and the other arm vise-gripped around my body. I felt my feet leave the ground as he overpowered me and we headed to the outside door.

He gestured to the others to follow. Physically, I was no match for them. I was pushed outside against my will. Someone broke a bottle just as we were exiting, and everyone's attention turned to them. No one noticed him dragging me out.

Outside, I felt vulnerable and I panicked. I struggled to break free, but it was no use. The guys were drunk and mean. One held me against the car with his hand clamped tightly over my mouth. His hands tasted of sweat and smelled of smoke; it nauseated me. He opened his car door, shoved me in, slammed, and locked the door. Why weren't my friends looking for me by now?

A strange calm came over me. I listened to what they were saying. I blocked out the noise and only listened.

One guy said, "Where're we supposed to take her and what can we do with her?"

Another answered, "I don't know, but we got five thousand bucks each to make sure that that one…" he pointed at the car I was in. "…is missing for a while. Someone needs her brothers to come looking for her. They want to get them alone. We need to get her out of here."

"Why?" Another said.

The second one answered, "I don't care. I didn't ask a lot of questions. Five thousand bucks is five thousand bucks. I can do a lot with that money. I was just told to get her and get her away from her brothers so they would come looking for her. I guess someone wants to get them out alone somewhere. Look I really don't know, I'm just guessing. All I know is this is the easiest five thousand bucks I ever made. Must be a beef with her brothers."

The guy who had thrown me in the car shrugged. "We got the girl in the car—as far as I'm concerned she's ours now. We've earned our money. If these guys got problems with her brothers, they ain't gonna care what we do with her, right? I say let's have some fun. Do what we want. She's a wildcat and a looker. Then we dump her on the highway afterwards and take off. Course if we do this, we'll need to leave town. I ain't doing no jail time. We'll scare her into not telling at least for a while, long enough for us to collect our money and skip town. Look…" They leered through the window at me. "She's so scared. She won't say anything."

"My car's here too." A different guy unlocked his car with his key.

The guy who had dragged me out laughed. "I'll drive her, you follow. I'll call you and let you know how my *date* went." With that he looked back at me and then back at the other two guys. "Then both you can have your *date*."

I had to do something! I couldn't let them take me out of this parking lot. I concentrated on Jorden. "*Help! Parking lot. Bring a lot of guys.*"

I thought it over and over again, twenty times at least. I heard a thump on the car. I closed my eyes. Tears streamed down my face, but I kept sending the message to Jorden.

The car door opened. Someone pulled me into his arms. "I'm here, Sis."

"Jorden." I hugged his neck and cried. "You heard me?"

He sat me down on the car seat. "Yes."

Police sirens screamed. Heath rubbed my hair. I buried my face in his chest and sobbed uncontrollably.

Who paid huge dollars to get my brothers *out of the way*? Who had that kind of money? A cold chill ran down my spine as I thought of all the rich people I knew. Who was the wealthiest?

Heath's Dad.

Did I honestly believe he had anything to do with all of this?

Was it all connected?

What did it all mean?

Chapter 30

As I entered Biology class, Clay excitedly noted, "We're starting our first cut on Brad the Bod today."

"Yeah," I said a little less than enthusiastically. Two murder attempts had been made; somebody was definitely after my brothers.

Clay and I stood over the fake cadaver we had named Brad as an homage to a current movie star. The other two in our group, Beth and Patra, didn't seem the least bit interested.

I handed the scalpel to Clay. "You can take the first cut."

"Really?" He wasted no time. Perhaps he thought that I might change my mind. He proceeded with the Y-cut precisely sliced down the drawn guide. Our lab had a microphone just like in a real autopsy room.

Clay spoke into the microphone. "Brad the Bod is a thirty-two year old male who died of unknown causes. It is our job to find out what insidious consequence befell this man in the prime..." Patra rolled her eyes.

Clay quit talking, consulted the manual, and began again. "Making the first incision..."

Clay tried to jump ahead, but was quickly halted by the professor. It was the only step we completed.

Clay was on cloud nine. "Thanks for letting me do that. Did you see the skin and tissues, and the heart?"

Clay could hardly contain his excitement. "I know there was supposed to be little blood but I didn't believe it, I thought it'd be

160

gushing out all over. Wow! This is like the real thing, blood and all. This school didn't scrimp on anything. Unbelievable! Thanks for letting me go first. "

I stored our equipment. "Sure."

I heard Clay say, "You were so into it I thought you wouldn't let me have a turn at all."

I turned to face him. "Why would you think I wouldn't let you have a turn?"

He seemed confused. "I didn't say anything."

"You didn't?" I sat down hard on the rolling metal chair in a lopsided way, which caused it to go flying across the room and me to fall on the floor with a thump.

"You okay?" He helped me up. Confused, I was thankful for the distraction.

I sat quietly pretending to get over the fall and concentrated, trying not to look at him or make it too obvious.

I had heard Clay's voice, but his lips weren't moving. I was hearing the second voice!

I smirked as I heard, "Sometimes you are one weird chick, Leah."

It was *The Voice. The Voice* I'd been hearing was the second voice. I tried the gift a few more times in other classes. It seemed to be hit or miss. Mostly misses. Kelly was worried my brother was going to dump her. I had never realized how insecure she was.

I discovered some of my friends' secret fears and anxieties. Jane worried about her looks. Constance obsessively worried about her weight and she was in love with Heath, no big surprise there. Patra didn't always like Constance, which *was* a surprise. Beth wished she could autopsy the plastic cadaver, but she was scared to say so. Clay worried he would be dumped, and many people felt big pressure to be perfect and get all A's. I wished some of the things they worried about were all I had to worry about.

The newfound ability made me completely forget about Grandma Jewell.

"I've been looking for you." Heath trotted towards me and

grabbed my arm. "Car's running. Tuesday, remember?"

"Oh yeah." I dashed to his vehicle. I tried unsuccessfully to hear Heath. I wondered if that would be true for all members of the Bolcan family. I'd like to try it on Mr. Bolcan.

I hurried to Grandma's room and seized my opportunity to do a trial run. I concentrated on Grandma. Nothing. I tried again. Nothing. Maybe it didn't work on the Bolcans.

She opened the book, carefully licking her fingers to find her desired page. "We need to work on the second voice today."

I stopped her. "Grandma, there have been two attempts on my brothers. Does that have anything to do with any of this?" I watched her, intending to listen to what she said, but I heard something else— two voices simultaneously communicating. One seemed to be a brush-off. I tuned that voice out and listened to the other one.

Grandma's second voice said, "There is a dark secret, but you're not ready."

"Dark secret?"

Grandma's eyes got big. By the look on her face, she'd realized my powers were expanding.

The second unspeaking voice of Grandma said, "I have to quit thinking or I'll tell her about the other locked book on the shelf behind me."

I got up and walked over to the shelf. I rubbed my hand across the spines of books and waited for her to tell me in unspoken word which book was the right one, and she did. I pulled a large pasteboard covered book off the shelf and brought it to the table. Like the original book, this book's cover had a star drawn, but it was different. A snake shaped the star. I recognized the star—it was the star tattoo.

"Your gifts have grown." She uncomfortably sighed. "I guess it's not my place to decide when you're ready. Your gift has decided you need to know." She frowned at me. "This part is not very pleasant. I wasn't sure if you could handle all of this. I haven't tried to hide it from you."

I wished I could believe her, but the second voice betrayed her. I needed to know what she knew. No matter how crazy all of this was,

I *was* involved and involved in a big way.

I touched her hand. "Please tell me the truth—the whole truth."

A flash of fear blasted through her eyes. "I will." She pulled a star-shaped key from around her neck. She unlocked the clasp on the book with her key. "Are you ready?"

I nodded. I was as ready as I would ever be.

She started. "I told you about the star points." She drew the outline of the star again. "Hawaii, Aleutian Islands, Alaska, Canada, and Berry to finish." I nodded and she drew dots on the points. "What I didn't tell you is that there are divisions within our group. They formed hoping to bring the prophecy to fruition earlier than destined. They are unaware that the prophecy has begun. Some clans have been infiltrated by evil. There is an immoral faction within the clans and they will do anything to inherit the gifts."

I stared at her. "What does that have to do with the attempts on my brothers?'

I listened to her voice and her second voice; she was telling me the truth. "I believe this evil splinter group is responsible for the havoc befalling your brothers. They draw their star with a serpent. They follow a different path."

I stared at her wide-eyed. "Different path?"

She started again. "Over the centuries there have been many truces between the clans and the evil groups." She turned the page and written at the top was Lava Bands.

I pointed to it. "What does this mean?"

Grandma Jewell's hands formed a circle. "The clans thought that the Earth represented the souls of their people. The bright souls were from the Sky and Star Clans—the dreamers. The grounded, realistic clans were the Island and Volcano Clans. The Water Clan represented a glue of sorts that held the clans together."

She paused for a moment, and then continued, "The clans who broke from their original tribes went to the inner places. These lineage lines had some gifts, but their genetic line skewed. Their powers lessened throughout the centuries. They had no true leader,

163

no healing powers, and no profound gifts. They are the weakest link to the ancient ones. Their belief is that this is their time to triumph and if they stop the prophecy, they will inherit the powers. The gifts will pass to them. I think this is why your brothers are being targeted. They fear your brothers will fulfill the prophecy."

I asked, "Why?"

"Because the clans and bands have begun to gather in one place and the stars are aligned. All the signs point to an upheaval. The inner factions are fearful and think if they wipe out the threat of the prophecy, it will cease to exist, and they will inherit the power."

"What can be done?" I asked her. "Do you know where they're located?"

She turned the page. "No, I don't know where. The prophecy states there will be a great battle. There is no prediction as to which group will survive."

I asked. "So everyone is either in Berry now or will come to Berry?"

She nodded.

I continued, "The men who tried to hurt me to get to my brothers received a large sum of money. I'm hoping the police will be able to trace it."

She patted my hand. "I'm glad the police are looking into this, but if this person has that much money at his disposal, then he probably has good ways to hide it."

"True. So what can we do?"

She rubbed my hair. "We have to develop your gifts. What is keeping you safe now is that no one knows about your powers."

I asked. "How do we really know what part I play?"

She smiled. "We don't. We can't know for sure. I hope I'm doing the right thing for our future."

I looked at her. "So that's all?"

She lied. "Yes."

Her second voice said, "There's one more thing."

Chapter 31

I grabbed Grandma's hand before she shut the book. "One more thing. Show me."

Her head dropped. She turned slowly to the very last page. It was entitled "The Secret of the Bloodstone."

"My ruby," I murmured. "What does it say?" I touched her hand. "I'll know if you're lying."

She nodded. "The bloodstone is prophesied to show the way to the fountain. After the bloodstone shows the way, if the heir of the bloodstone drinks from the fountain at the proper time—" She stopped and gazed at me.

 "What happens?"

She read, "They will inherit a great power and life will be beautiful on planet earth for the next three thousand years."

I tapped again. "And if not?"

She sighed. "If not, it will set up a chain reaction and will set in motion a series of events that will change the outcome. It does not give specifics about what will happen. But it alludes that life will be difficult. Nature will be askew. Balance lost. Earthquakes, famine, hurricanes, all sorts of natural phenomenon and disasters will happen. The world will be out of kilter."

"So finding this fountain first is important and making sure the right person drinks from it at the right time and we don't know where it is or how to find it or who should drink out of it, right?"

She nodded. "And keeping the fountain's whereabouts secret is very important too."

"Anything else in that book?"

She pointed to the book. "There is a time constraint and some other specifics."

"*Of course there is*," I replied sarcastically. "And that is?"

She trailed her finger across the writing. "It's about who to marry..."

"Stop. I don't want to know; it might make a difference to me. I don't want to make a fortune come true simply by hearing it. I don't want to alter events. I want to choose my path. At least I know now that I need to find out where students at Berry come from to see if I notice any patterns."

She nodded. "I guess."

I wrote all of this down. "That'll help. I need to do some investigative work. Any instructions on how to use the bloodstone, ruby thing?"

She surveyed the book again. "No, it just says it will show the way."

I smiled at her. "I've had no vibrating. Maybe I don't have the right ruby."

I hated to ask the next question, but I needed to know. "Is Mr. Bolcan involved in any of this?"

She looked straight into my eyes. "Not in any way that you think. We're all involved."

She was telling the truth.

I had a lot to think about and I still had homework. I laughed to myself. I didn't think this was the way a normal fifteen-year-old's life was supposed to go. But my life was far from normal.

The next day at school, I put my plan to find out where everyone was from into action. "Kelly, do you know where the gala committee meets and when?"

"The gala committee. Why?"

I tried to act as nonchalant as I could. "I had a great idea."

"What?"

166

"I was thinking that the gala needed a theme."

Kelly looked confused. "They already have a theme. They've had a theme for about a month. It's been announced."

I frowned. "Really?"

"Around the World in four short hours." Kelly put her hand under her chin. "We're going to have buffet lines of food from different countries and have our gala pictures taken in front of backdrops representing different locations like Paris' Eiffel Tower."

I moved in close as she talked, trying my best to look interested. What luck! The theme suited my purpose. "What do you think about the idea that since we all come from different places that as we come in—we get a flag pin that represents the country or state we come from?"

"Really inventive." She jumped up. "The committee will love that idea. How cute! What made you think of it?"

I lied. "I don't know." I glanced down and then back at her. "Hey, you want to go to the committee and present the idea? Take credit. I don't care."

She shook her head at me. "I don't want to take your idea as my own."

"Look." I sat her down on the bench outside the Media Center. "I really have a lot on my plate right now, and if I go and tell them about this they'll want me to help with making the pins—"

She squealed. "I love to do stuff like that."

I nodded. "I know you do. It would be a great favor to me if you would go and present this as your idea."

She jumped up and hugged me. "They don't have any sophomores. I might get voted to head the committee for next year."

She ran off, turned around, and came back and hugged me hard again. "Thanks again, Leah. You're the best!"

I smiled. Now everyone would walk around with flags of countries or states where they came from. It ought to give me some place to start. That night I started brushing up on my geography and the flags.

167

Finally, the big night arrived. Our moms insisted we dress at our own houses to get family pictures before ending up at our house to get the group shots. It was a bustling night at the Skye household. I slipped into my gala dress. Light mascara, pink gloss and a smidge of blue eyeliner with matching shadow and a cascade of curls completed my look.

Once again, Heath supplied the limousine. Blue brought Kate. We took single pictures, couple pictures, group pictures, just the boys, just the girls, inside and outside pictures.

After over an hour of taking and posing for pictures, I tapped my watch. "We're going to miss the gala if we don't go now."

As we arrived at the hall, the welcoming committee sat in front of a long table. It was filled with every kind of flag you could think of. I was amazed at the myriad of colors and symbol combos—ones with two stars, one star, stripes every which way, all the colors of the spectrum. There were so many flags Heath and I had trouble finding ours—Hawaii and Florida.

He pinned the Florida flag on me. "Not too exotic."

I chuckled. "I've lived here all my life."

I had a plan. I would spend the night looking for those flags. After all, I'd memorized all of them.

Photographers grabbed couples as they entered. I rolled my eyes. "More pictures." We posed and then did a few goofy ones before we made it into the actual hall.

Entering the dance area, I could see a lot of work had gone into the decorations. The area was divided into different countries' motifs. Stations depicting the Eiffel Tower of Paris, Statue of Liberty of New York, Taj Mahal of India, the Pyramids and Sphinx of Egypt, the Big Wall of China, a Venetian background complete with a gondola, Germany's Neuschwanstein Castle, a couple of decorations with Asian flavor, a bullfighting arena, and a kangaroo and the Sydney Opera House from Australia enhanced the international theme.

Heath took me by the arm. "We need to find our seat."

Printed place cards with names stood on each table. "We have assigned seats?"

Jane grinned. "That was my idea." She ran to the front of the dance floor. "I know right where we are. We got one of the best tables in the room." She pointed to a table behind a column. "That's Constance's table, there were *some* perks to doing all this work." She giggled and I smiled. Jane surprised me, she did have a little touch of mean.

Locating everyone's flags was going to be harder than I imagined. I had planned to watch the people in front of me, but now we were in the front. Still, I had four hours to accomplish my mission.

Once we located our seats, we went to the buffet tables. Tea and water were served at the tables. It was hard to pick, so I tried to get a little pinch of everything. I loaded my plate with a French baguette, a small piece of a Coney Island hot dog, rasgulla from India (surprisingly cheesy and sweet), Egyptian koshary (mixture of pasta, rice, lentil, chick peas, onions, garlic and chili sauce), little German sausages, arroz con pollo, a little fried rice and topped it off with a fortune cookie. I had more food than an army could eat.

"Oh! Sorry!" exclaimed a waiter as he inadvertently spilled water on my plate. I was glad—an excuse to not to stuff myself.

I hadn't been able to mingle to see if I recognized any flags before the music had started. The lights dimmed as the band played the first few songs to an empty dance floor.

Kelly pulled me onto the center of the floor. "We need to get this party started."

We bopped to the tunes, which prompted a few more girls to join us. The guys started dancing and by the time another song started, the floor was full.

"I'm feeling a little woozy." I put my hand on Heath's shoulder. "I think I need to sit down. Too much food or too much moving."

Heath walked me unsteadily over to the table. "Me too."

We both sat and put our heads down.

Blue came over from his assigned table next to us. "Kate's not feeling well. I'm taking her home."

I surveyed the area. People started to sway—a couple even fell and crawled back to their seats. The dance floor was sparse except for a few people crazily dancing all around.

I stared at Blue. "How do you feel?"

Nervously, Blue's eyes darted from one end of the hall to the other. "I'm okay," he mumbled.

Jorden had joined us by now. He put his hands on each of our shoulders trying to steady himself. "I'm feeling it too, Leah." He leaned into Blue. "Whatd'ya drink tonight?"

"I brought my juice from home. You know the protein stuff." Blue picked up my glass and smelled. "Do you think someone spiked the punch?"

I fell back in my chair down unable to stand. "I think someone spiked the tea and water." Nauseated, I placed my head down.

Blue put a hand on me and one on Jorden. "You guys stay here. I gotta get my girl and the people I came with home safely. I'll be back for you. Don't try to drive. Just hang tight." He looked around. "In fact, I'll bring Mom and Dad and some more help."

I waved him on as a wave of nausea made my head goose bump. "Good idea."

By this time everyone at my table was sitting and moaning. The elixir had distinctively differing effects on people. Some were giddy. I tried to identify people not affected. Should be the culprits.

A boy scaled the Eiffel Tower and banged his chest like King Kong. The tower fell with a thud, injuring some bystanders below. Unfortunately, no one could help. Others tried to ride in the gondola, which tipped over as one boy sang an Italian song. He kept singing as he sprawled out sideways on the floor.

One boy talked to the stuffed kangaroo. "You're pretty, do you want to go out sometime?"

A girl banged on the fake door at the castle. "Prince, are you in there?" Another girl walked up and they fought over the nonexistent Prince Charming.

Wild scenarios like those played out all around the hall.

I heard a conversation between two unfamiliar boys, one with a serpent tattoo on his wrist. I could only distinguish a few words. "...

truth serum…effect soon…in the tea and water …hangover."

Truth serum.

Oh no! I'm in trouble.

Chapter 32

I realized I was using my gift to hear them. I was in no shape to fully discern what they were saying. Blue lifted Kate up and carried her out.

I smiled. "Blue sure does love Kate." I sounded drunk.

Heath lifted his head up. "He'd do anything for Kate. Just like I'd do anything for you, Leah." He tried to kiss me.

I backed away. "Heath, quit it."

I heard feet stomping up.

"Leah!" A male voice bellowed over me. It was Stone.

His appearance and manner made me uncomfortable. "Don't you know that I've been trying to get you to go out with me from day one?" He knelt down beside me. "I can't seem to get you between boyfriends. First, it was that Eskimo-loving boy, Q or W, or something. Then he left. I thought, now I'll ask her out. You went for a Neanderthal." He shot a thumb towards Heath. "This clown."

Heath staggered up. "Who you calling a clown?" His words slurred together. He swung at Stone, but fell on the ground.

Stone pushed his shirtsleeve up and flexed his muscles. "You're no match for me. I'm the strongest man in school. Look, Leah. Look." With that last statement, Stone passed out too.

It would have been humorous, had I not been so scared of spilling the beans about something I shouldn't. Outlandish situations happened all over.

I listened to see if anyone made sense.

One brother said to another, "Remember the time you got

blamed for stealing the car?"

His brother commented. "Yeah?"

"It was me, I felt bad that you got in trouble."

His brother was infuriated. "Mom and Dad made me stay the night in jail. Why didn't you own up to that?"

"I don't know."

The two started yelling about other secrets. Everyone was out of control.

A girl told her friend. "I'm in love with Alan. I've always loved Alan and hated you because he's your boyfriend." A shouting match followed. Confessions, confrontations, arguments, and silliness occurred everywhere.

One teacher said to the principal, "You're so stupid. My teaching certificate is forged and you never checked. I never went to college. I barely graduated high school. You're one stupid principal." He collapsed. I wondered if they'd remember in the morning.

One of the teachers' wives confessed. "I lost my job a month ago and I've been going to the park every day when I'm supposed to be at work." She started crying.

I gushed at Kelly. "I love you, Kelly."

I leaned over to Jane. "I love you, Jane."

We cried all over each other.

"We love you too." They said, "We're best friends."

I sat there bawling. I tried to be strong. I had secrets, but I was determined not to tell them.

I heard an unknown voice that did not sound affected. "Where's Jorden?"

Another voice I didn't recognize answered. "We'll find him and see if he knows anything. He'll tell us.'"

I was scared. Jorden could tell them about the gifts and me. I had to do something.

I saw Jorden as he was picked up by his feet and hands. Both guys had star tattoos. I concentrated.

I tried to send him a message. "Jorden, the guys who are dragging you are bad. Don't let them get you outside." I concentrated as hard as I could.

I heard him. "What can I do?"

I concentrated. "I don't know— do something!"

Thump! Jorden hit the floor.

One man said, "He threw up on me!"

Another one responded, "We need him."

The other man huffed off. "Count me out."

I leaned up and saw a man drag Jorden by his ankle. I didn't know what to do. Heath and Stone stirred. I wasn't above anything to save my brother.

I staggered to my feet, bumping into a few chairs. I knocked someone over before I finally reached Heath and Stone. I grabbed them by their collars, one in each hand. "If you love me, truly love me, then you'll bring Jorden to me now."

They stared at me.

I yelled. "Prove your love. I want Jorden now!" I kept screaming. "Now! Now!"

Everything went black.

I woke up in my bedroom with my head pounding. I tried to stand, but my legs felt like jelly.

Terra bopped in. "You okay, Leah?"

I grabbed my head. "No reason to yell." I rushed into the bathroom. The toilet became my friend as I got rid of the food I'd eaten and most of the inside of my stomach.

It was well into the next evening before I ventured out. Downstairs, Mom and Dad were watching television.

Dad helped me into a chair. "You okay, Leah?"

I decided to play dumb. "What happened?"

Mom and Dad told me how Blue had brought Kate to the house and they went back with him to the hall to get everyone home. The police analyzed the tea and found sodium amytal—truth serum.

I asked, "Why would someone do that?"

My mother said, "I have no idea, or where someone would get that from. Sodium amytal is a controlled substance. It must have been stolen."

Dad glanced over at her. "The kids who stole it probably didn't know what it was, just mixed the drugs with liquor, and thought it'd be funny."

"Did they catch anyone?"

They both shook their heads.

I needed the answer to one more question. "Did I say anything bizarre?"

Mom laughed. "What didn't you say that was weird? When we got you in the car, you said all kinds of crazy things...what was some of it, Hon?" She looked over at my Dad.

Dad put his hand under his chin. "Something about a prophecy and hearing voices and Jorden being in trouble."

Mom interrupted. "Yeah, that was most of it. You were worried about Jorden—very sweet." She kissed me on my forehead. "Don't worry. It was just us. Jorden said silly things too."

"So everything's okay? I'm not in trouble or anything?" I studied them, trying to gauge their reaction.

She grinned. "Of course, you're not in trouble. We know it wasn't your fault. Just a vicious prank. The doctor said to give you two a couple of days to recuperate."

"A doctor? What doctor?"

"Someone the school sent. Said his kids went to the school—I didn't know him—Dr. Thomas. Related to Kate somehow. He seemed nice." She turned back to her television show. "Get some rest. Everything will be back to normal in a couple of days."

I had been full of truth serum, this could still be bad.

What had I told this doctor?

Chapter 33

Monday at school was strange. People remembered bits and pieces. The teacher who had confessed was fired. Heath and Stone didn't speak to each other for a while. Then they acted like best buddies trying to cover for their whole "fight" thing; I think they were embarrassed. We had a big assembly and I saw Dr. Thomas.

I whispered to Kate. "Are you related?"

She whispered. "Some sort of long distance way. He is Beth and L.H.'s Dad. We're third cousins."

"Interesting." The fact that Dr. Thomas was related to someone I knew made me feel a little better—not sure why.

Dr. Thomas told us to forget what we had said and what had been said to others. He made a big speech about how people with lost inhibitions could fabricate stories. We should just ignore what had happened. The school deputy asked anyone with information to come forward as soon as possible.

I decided to put it all behind me—finals were close. The end of the school year was fast approaching and I had to figure out something to do for the summer.

In dance class that week, Stone sat beside me. "I've got to go to a family wedding this weekend at Secret Lake. Would you go with me?"

I wondered if it was a good idea after what I had heard at the gala.

He started again. "I asked Heath and he said you should go

with me and you were free to do what you wanted to do."

Surprised, I stared at him. I tried to see if the secret voice was in play. I couldn't tell. "He said that?"

Stone nodded.

Might be fun getting out of town for a while. "Sure. I guess. I'll have to ask my folks, but I don't see a problem with it. I love weddings."

He smiled. "I'll be by to pick you up about three-thirty. The wedding's at five."

I nodded. Heath was sticking to our pact to be just friends. I liked that.

I saw Heath at lunch. "Stone asked me to go to a wedding with him this weekend. He said he talked to you about it."

Heath looked puzzled then said, "Oh he asked me to go with him. I told him to take a girl. I didn't know he'd ask you."

I studied him. "You don't mind, do you?"

"Of course not. I feel bad I knocked him out at the gala. I know I'm a boyfriend-in-waiting."

Selective memory was an interesting phenomenon.

That Saturday, I put on a yellow sundress and sandals. I figured if it were fancy or simple, the dress would work.

Stone spoke to my parents and then grinned at me. "You look beautiful." I could tell this wasn't just a friend thing to him.

In his car, he adjusted the mirror. "It's about an hour to the wedding. It's on a plantation a little ways past Secret Lake."

I smiled. "I haven't been out this way in a while. My great-grandmother used to live near Secret Lake."

"Really." He acted interested in every word I said. "Tell me more."

Stone and I talked about our families. It had been Chloe and then three boys so they were looking forward to another girl.

He touched my hand. "We're about ten minutes away."

A high-pitched sound made me shudder. "Do you hear that?'

He looked around. "No. What?"

He obviously didn't hear it. "Oh…nothing. I thought I heard something."

It got louder. I pretended to pay attention to his conversation, but I wanted to know where the noise was coming from.

"Oh!" An electric-like pulse jolted me.

"You okay?" Stone asked when I jerked.

I nodded. The jolt came from my ruby, the bloodstone, and if legend rang true that meant the fountain was very close. Close enough to trigger the bloodstone.

Chapter 34

"**H**ey Stone." I flirted.

He grinned. "Yeah."

I batted my eyes. "On the way home could we drive around? I'd like to see if I recognize any of the old places I used to go to with my family."

"Sure."

We pulled into the plantation.

I wasn't looking forward to this. I'd be thinking about the fountain the whole time. First, the wedding, and then the fountain. I'd get there. Right now, I needed to be patient.

We were late and had to sneak in the back. We slid into the groom's side. I assumed that was Stone's side of the family. The wedding was beautiful. The bride cried and the groom messed up his vows. Stone put his hand over mine at the kiss. Yes, this was more than just a friend thing to him.

We ate dinner and danced under a big tent. Stone introduced me to his family as his girlfriend. I didn't correct him.

Finally, we said our good-byes and started home.

I reminded him. "Remember we're going to drive around."

He put his hand on mine. "Sure."

"Turn down this road." The bloodstone vibrated and the sound grew louder and more intense. I grabbed the necklace as it suddenly lifted off my chest toward the left. "Is there a turn off to the left here?"

"Yeah." Stone turned down a dirt road.

The road circled and curved. We followed it as far as we could.

"Are you sure you know where you are going? " Stone frowned at me. "I don't want to get lost."

I was lying so much I was making myself sick. "Yeah, there's a pond here. I'm sure it's up this road."

We went deeper into an area with no visible signs of civilization. I didn't even know there were such places still in Florida, but here we were. The road finally ended. Stone stopped the car and turned off the engine.

He leaned over and put his arm around me. "Now what do you want to do?"

I tried to hide my surprise. He had it wrong, but I *had* asked a boy on what he thought was a date to take me to a secluded place.

I fidgeted uncomfortably. "Well it's our first date. I don't think we ought to—"

He seemed embarrassed. "I wasn't planning on it. I thought..."

I realized what this looked like. "I honestly didn't want to get us lost and wasn't trying to lead you on. I must have remembered something wrong."

I gazed at him sweetly. "Sorry."

"That's okay." He smiled. "I'm glad you called it a date." Even though it was dark, I could see him turn red.

He clarified. "I thought it was a date. I didn't know if you thought of it as a date."

I wanted to change the subject. "Do you mind if we get out and look around?"

He leaned over me, opened up the glove compartment, and pulled out a flashlight.

I scooted over to his side of the car to get out after him. "Good idea. It's kind of dark."

He shone the flashlight. "There's a trail."

"Can we go down it a bit?" I asked.

He nodded. "We can go down it a little ways, maybe fifteen minutes. We don't want to get lost on our first *date*."

Down the trail, the sound got louder and the ruby vibrated

more. I knew I was close. I walked a couple of steps behind Stone. The ruby illuminated.

He flinched. "What was that?"

I asked innocently. "What?"

"I thought I saw a flash of red light." He circled his flashlight around. I backed up a couple of steps. The ruby stopped glowing.

We were close, but I couldn't chance it. I didn't want to have to explain. I'd memorize this place and come back with Blue or Jorden.

"I think you're right. I really do think I took a wrong turn." I looked around. "I don't recognize anything and it's starting to get really dark."

Fortunately, he accepted that explanation. It took a while to find our way back to the main road.

On the hour-long trip back, we talked about the wedding, our families, and school. My mind wandered as I thought about the fountain and the ruby's trigger.

Stone walked me to the door and leaned in for a kiss.

I embraced him instead. "Thanks, I really had a good time." And I meant it.

I flipped on my computer to search the area at Secret Lake. I planned to look at the satellite map to see if I could see the fountain. Automatically, my unread email messages appeared so I opened them first.

There was another email from Mr. Lant's assistant trying to locate me to give me something. I deleted it. A few messages from my friends that I opened and read.

I hadn't checked my spam in about a month. It was loaded. At first, I selected delete all, but decided to take a quick look—every once in a while somebody I needed to hear from ended up in spam. I scrolled down the list. The next to the last email was from an address I didn't recognize. The subject caught my eye—*heart anklet*.

Chapter 35

*H*eart anklet. I stared at the subject. Could it be? My heart started pounding. Z? The date on the email was from over a month ago.

I clicked it to be delivered. In a few minutes, it came on my email.

Leah. I'm forbidden to contact you. I am sending this off another's email. I'm sorry but you can't write me back. Getting vibes you are in danger. Be careful. Z

Forbidden. Who forbade him? My mind raced. I tried to remember the time when this email was sent. Were we in Hawaii? Maybe. When I thought of Z, I couldn't catch my breath. I shut my eyes and tried to remember exactly where I had been the exact day he had sent this. My mind clouded. I couldn't think straight.

Was he engaged? I'd heard that. Could it be true? Why didn't he call me? What if he was engaged? Who gets married at sixteen? Tears streamed down my cheeks.

How could I let him get to me this way again? I had given him my heart. I had been closer to him than I'd ever been to anyone. And he had left me. He left me cold. I felt like my arm had been ripped off. He betrayed me. He left me. What a pitiful excuse for an email message!

NO!

NO!

NO!

NOT AGAIN!!

I don't know how long I sat there staring at my laptop. How could he still get to me? I hadn't seen him in months, not since my birthday. Could I be so angry I couldn't think straight?

I centered my emotions, definitely a drawback for heightened senses. I felt intensely both ways—negatively and positively. My soul anguished.

I finally dried my tears and climbed into bed too exhausted to care about searching for the fountain. Maybe tomorrow.

It took two weeks to talk Jorden and Blue into riding to Secret Lake with me. During that time, there were no more attempts on my brothers' lives. I pushed my thoughts of Z far back into the recesses of my mind. I refused to think about him. Even now, it hurt too much.

I decided to do a high school internship at Lake Hospital. I'd spend two weeks in each of five departments: obstetrics, the surgical floor, urgent care, intensive care, and neonatal.

Since I had returned from spring break, I had improved with my powers each week in my lessons with Grandma Jewell. I learned to control some of my gifts. If I spent a minute tuning out the outside, I could hear conversations in other buildings.

I felt I should keep the bloodstone and its vibration, humming sound, and glowing at Secret Lake a secret from Grandma. I reasoned I didn't want to get her hopes up, but I wasn't a hundred percent sure, I could trust Grandma.

Who did I trust?

My family.

Period.

I wanted to find out if Blue had any abilities and how powerful Jorden's gifts were.

Nothing from Z. I hated myself for it, but I checked my email every day. Maybe I was just a glutton for punishment. I'd start thinking—he might be married or have a baby on the way...STOP... I would tell myself... and I'd listen to myself most of the time.

Blue met us at the car. "Now where are we going and why?"

I climbed in the backseat. "Trust me, Blue. No questions, you'll understand when we get there." I winked at Jorden who climbed in the front seat.

Blue caught my wink. "Oh, a surprise. I love surprises." He relaxed as excitement filled his eyes. Blue did love a mystery.

We talked the whole hour over to Secret Lake about my internship and Blue's college plans. He planned on walking on the Florida State University football team. He talked about Kate and seemed to have his whole life planned out. Jorden talked some about Kelly.

I tapped Jorden's shoulder. "Do you hear the noise?'

He nodded.

Blue glanced back at me. "I hear humming. Is that what you're talking about?'

"Yeah." I smiled—he did have some of the gifts. What else had Blue been keeping from us?

I nodded. "Follow the noise."

Blue cocked his head. "Why?"

"Just humor me, okay?"

Blue shrugged, but followed the noise anyway. I think he was curious to find out what this was all about. Jorden asked no questions.

Sunlight flooded the meadow's clearing and I wasn't sure if I would be able to see the ruby's light if it glowed.

I saw the field where Stone and I had been. "We're here."

Blue stopped the car. "Where?"

We all got out.

I motioned to Jorden. "Did you bring flashlights?"

"Why do we need flashlights with the sun—" Jorden mumbled as he popped the trunk and retrieved three flashlights.

"Maybe we won't, but just in case."

Jorden handed us each a flashlight. "Be prepared—boy scout's code."

"Follow the sound." I walked ahead and the other two followed me.

We didn't have to go far before the ruby glowed, not a problem

184

to see. It lit up the whole forest and guided us.

Blue's eye lit up. "I'm interested now so much so that I'm not even going to ask what this is all about. I have a sneaking suspicion that I'm going to find out very soon."

When I made a wrong turn, the ruby's light would dim. We walked in complete silence for well over an hour. The stone's illumination kept growing. It seemed to be the most intense in one spot. I stood where it was the brightest; if I moved a step in any direction, it dimmed.

"This must be the spot." I surveyed the area. I saw no fountain or anything that remotely looked like a water source. "It's not here." I remarked disappointedly.

"What?" Blue asked. "What exactly are we looking for?'

"A fountain," I said dejectedly.

He stopped abruptly. "Why didn't you say so?" He motioned for us to come with him.

I shot a confused look to Jorden. We shrugged, but followed.

We trailed Blue down a path as the ruby dimmed. I had no answers; maybe Blue did. I hoped Blue did.

Blue pushed some of the vegetation to the side with his foot. "It's here somewhere." He picked up a branch and started poking and prodding.

I stood by him shining the light where he was digging. "What?"

He pushed away some more brush. "You wanted to see the fountain. Right?"

I grabbed Blue's arm, "Do you know where the fountain is?"

"Of course. Gamma's fountain." He shoved some more brush back and uncovered a small opening. "Here it is. Follow me."

Blue laughed. "I was much smaller then." Filthy from the dig, he pulled his shirt off exposing his semi-clean undershirt. "We're gonna get dirty." He used the branch to make the opening bigger.

Jorden removed his outer shirt and I was glad I had worn jeans and tennis shoes. I hadn't planned on a grimy outdoor adventure. Blue led the way. Jorden pushed me through easily and followed. We squeezed through the dirt tunnel as our flashlights illuminated the way. We crawled for about ten feet on our elbows and flat on our tummies. Finally, I felt myself fall. Blue caught me and I stood up in a cave of some sort. Jorden tumbled in after and landed on the cave floor.

Blue ran ahead. "I can't believe I remember this place."

As we walked back through the cave, the ruby glowed stronger. I realized I had been standing above this cave when the ruby had glowed. We were heading to the source. My heart beat faster. The three of us trotted while our flashlights danced up and down on the cave walls.

We stopped.

There it was.

Chapter 36

Magnificently gushing in the middle of this secret underground cave was the most beautiful underwater spring I'd ever seen. A fissure housed in the ground spewed the shimmering liquid. The prism of water sparkled as a small bit of sunlight trickled through crevasses in the ground above. It was the most beautiful fountain I'd ever seen. It made its own sun catcher. The colors of red, blue, and yellow changed as the water shot up and down in a soothing rhythm. Enamored, I stopped dumbfounded listening to the melodic tone.

Blue hiked over to the fountain. "Gamma brought me here when I was little."

Jorden put his hand in the water.

"No!" Blue yelled. "Gamma said we must never drink the water."

Jorden pulled his hand back quickly. "Why? Is it poison?"

Blue frowned. "Not sure. Gamma said we couldn't drink it. I don't know why."

"Fine, no drinking." Jorden sat down on a seat made by a protrusion in the cave wall and watched the cascading water. "It's mesmerizing."

I remembered the prophecy stating only the right person should drink from the fountain so I agreed with Blue. We knew where it was now and we could come back whenever we wanted.

I said, "We need to make sure that no one but us knows this is here."

Blue sat on another seat made by the cave protrusion. "If

anyone else came here they'd be trespassing. Besides, who could find this place?"

As I inspected the cave room opening, I noticed there were five rock projections that seemed to make a room of chairs surrounding the fountain. The colors lit the room like a kaleidoscope strobe light filtered through water—colorful and surreal at the same time. It was like nothing I'd ever seen. The sweet smell was cinnamon, vanilla and the all too familiar smell of home—oranges.

I sat down on the rock chair next to Blue. "What'd ya mean?"

"Our family owns this area. Gamma owned this land. She left specific instructions that when she passed; it cannot be sold, built on, or anything. It's an ironclad document." Blue pointed around the cave. "We, the Skyes, own all of this."

Jorden mouthed the word "wow."

I looked at Blue. "How do you know all of this?"

Blue took a breath. "When I was young, I used to come here with Gamma and she'd read me stuff out of a big book. She said that I was the first born and needed to know about a prophecy about the Island…"

I finished "…of the Star."

Puzzled, he asked, "How do you know about that?"

"Heath's grandmother."

"Gamma said there were more than just us." He nodded his head. "You're getting the information from Heath's grandmother. Right? I thought there was something weird about you going over there once a week to read to her."

"She calls the weekly visits, lessons."

We smiled at each other. I was so happy I wasn't alone any more with all of this information. I wasn't the only one who knew about all of this.

I quizzed, "Where's the book now?"

"Not sure. I haven't seen it in a very long time." Blue scanned the cave. "Thought it might be in here, but don't see it."

The cave's walls were etched with drawings that seemed to be ancient. I outlined a few etchings with my finger. "These drawings seem to tell a story."

Jorden, who had been quietly listening, finally spoke. "Anybody want to clue me in?"

Blue, Jorden and I sat in the cave with the beautiful fountain and shared all that we knew about the prophecy. I told them about the five outer points of the star, the serpent star clan enemies along with the unrest and fight for control, and the ruby.

Jorden and I shared about our connections and the second voice. We talked in great detail about the two attempts on their lives.

Blue surmised that someone must think one of them was the one that the prophecy talked about.

Blue stated. "It could be any one of us."

I added. "Or none of us."

They both nodded.

Jorden blurted out. "My gifts have been getting stronger."

I agreed. "Mine too! Of course, I've been getting lessons."

Blue confessed he had powers of heightened senses. He'd been hiding them for a while.

Jorden asked me. "Do you think Grandma could give me lessons?"

"I'll ask her when I see her. I don't see why not."

Blue stood up. "Are you ready to leave the prism chasm?"

I asked, "What did you call it?"

"Gamma used to call it a prism chasm. She said that it was a prism because of the different colors and a chasm because of the deep crack that opened up to bring water to the surface." Blue turned and looked toward the opening. "I can't believe I remember all of this. I was just a little kid when I came here with her."

"Maybe the heightened senses help with memory too. I like that name. Prism Chasm." I took a long stroll around the room, trying to memorize the drawings. I'd bring a notebook next time. Maybe I could start my own Sky Clan book.

I noticed a drawing of what looked like five people inside a star; the figure in the middle had a gem on its head. The outer points of the star looked like pyramids. I inched closer and the ruby around

189

my neck that had been glowing the whole time started pulsating a myriad of colors—red, pink, purple, yellow, blue, green, then it abruptly stopped as I stood right in front of the figure drawing.

A single white light shot out of my ruby and fell upon the gem in the middle of the drawing and the rock opened like a drawer from the cave wall. "Did you see that?"

I didn't need an answer. I could feel Jorden and Blue hovering, their breath at each of my shoulders. "What should I do? Should I pull the rock?"

Nervous yeses followed as I gently grasped the rock; it came out easily. Blue grabbed it from me and laid it on the ground. I peered in behind the rock and there it sat covered in cobwebs— *The Book*.

Chapter 37

Jorden crowded in on one side. "What's in there?"

Blue peered in. "Gamma's book!"

I reached in, shoved the cobwebs aside, grabbed the book on each side, and freed it from its resting place. I sat it down gently on one of the rock protrusions. The three of us knelt beside it and surveyed it in astonishment.

"What does it say?" Jorden impulsively pulled at the cover, but it didn't budge. "It's stuck—it won't open."

Blue jerked Jorden's hand back. "Genius, it's probably locked. Look for a key in the opening. Leah, see if you can find a lock somewhere."

I searched the entire book and found no markings or clasps. "Shine the flashlight here—maybe the lock's on the front cover."

Blue shone the flashlight.

Jorden dropped a star-shaped metal piece on the rock beside the book. "This was the only other thing in that crevice."

"There's a star drawn on the cover and it recedes. Maybe it's the key." I placed the metal star in the shape and it fit snugly. My heart started pounding as I turned the star-shaped metal key, but it didn't budge.

"Something's missing." Blue gestured to Jorden. "Look carefully and make sure there was nothing else in there—maybe something dropped out."

Jorden spent a few minutes hunting in the cranny, but to no avail. We all three crawled around the dirt floor patting to find anything else. After a few minutes of searching, we all just sat on our knees silently.

I played with my necklace, trying to figure out what we were doing wrong when it suddenly came to me—the necklace. I unhooked the clasp and removed my ruby necklace. My brothers watched me. I placed the metal star-shaped key in its place, took the ruby off its chain, and laid it in the middle of the star. It didn't fit.

Blue waved his hand over the book. "Try it the other way."

I flipped over the ruby necklace and I twisted it slowly until it caught in place. I rotated the clasp—"click"— the book unlocked.

With all three of us packed close, I delicately turned to the first page. Jorden shone the light on its writings. The first page simply read: Sky Clan History. "Blue, hand me my backpack."

I opened the backpack and pulled out some latex gloves. "Put these on."

Jorden made a face. "Do you always carry gloves?"

"Of course." I smugly answered, "I'm going to be a doctor one day."

Blue snapped his gloves on his hands. "They came in handy today."

With the gloves on, I felt more at ease touching the book. I gently flipped to the next page. "This is a lot of the same stuff that's in Grandma Jewell's book."

"Compare the books. I didn't know she had a book too." Blue twirled his hand. "Go to the end see if there's anything different."

I gently turned the pages one by one, not wanting to tarry too long, afraid the boys might want me to stop and explain along the way. There was plenty of time for that later.

I stopped on an unfamiliar page. It read: Prophecy.

Blue put his latex-covered finger on the page. "Stop. That one I want to read."

"Me too." I nodded.

Jorden signaled a latex-gloved thumbs-up. "Unanimous."

"*BEWARE of the serpent star clan. Danger lurks as the prophecy begins.*

The generation of the prophecy begins after the light in the day sky disappears for 399 beats of a warrior's heart and the light in the night sky disappears on solstice."

"Gamma must have calculated this." Blue said as he pointed to the handwritten note 7/22/2009—Solar Eclipse for 6 minutes, 39 seconds—12/21/2010, Solstice Lunar Eclipse

I shuddered. "Our generation." I looked at the others and continued reading.

"There are three occurrences after the darkening of the day and night sky.

The first is that the ancestors of the Island of the Star clans and the Star of the East clans will gather at the same location near the fountain.

The second part is that children of the clans will discover their powerful gifts.

The third occurrence is that the middle child of the chosen family will come into possession of the bloodstone.

When all of these have occurred, the prophecy will engage. A great struggle will continue for many moons between the forces of good and evil. Sight, hearing, touch, taste, smell, second voice and other gifts will be revealed to the chosen and will be bestowed on the conquerors.

The prophecy states the two opposite clans must join forces to defeat the dark serpent star faction. By doing this the Island of the Star clans will be whole again. If this does not occur, then evil will triumph. The exceptional gifts bestowed in the beginning and taken away during the separation time will renew. As balance is restored, new gifts and powers will emerge. If the dark serpent faction prevails, the gifts will be bestowed upon them and balance will forever be lost."

I read the prophecy aloud two times. "Grandma Jewell says the clans are coming and I know our gifts are developing, but who is the second star clan from the East?"

Blue looked at me. "And who is the middle child?"

Jorden wrinkled his eyes. "Who is our middle child?"

I answered. "There isn't one, we're twins, and there are four of us. We're not the chosen family." I was relieved and looked at my necklace. "If this is the bloodstone, it must find its way into the rightful owner's hands."

Blue waved toward the cave opening. "It's getting dark. We gotta get back. Leah, lock the book and put it back. We'll come again. You find out what you can from Grandma Jewell. We have time; the final occurrence has not happened. But, we're still in danger. We have to be careful even if we're not the middle child or we're not the chosen family. It's important we keep this secret."

I shifted the book to close it and a piece of folded worn paper fell out. No one saw so I stuck it in my pocket. I'd bring it back later. I wanted a little piece of something to remind me this was real and not a dream. I closed the book, secured the clasp, removed my ruby, putting the necklace back around my neck, and gently placed the book back where it belonged. Blue replaced the rock and we locked the book back in its secret hiding place.

I shone my flashlight up toward the cave opening. "I think you're right— it might be darker than we thought. Hope we can find our way."

Blue started ahead. "I know I can. We need to cover the opening so no one can find it."

We inched our way out of the cave. At the opening, we found limbs and brush to cover it back up. Blue found his way easily back to the car. We drove home all the way talking. I felt so much safer knowing they knew of the prophecy and the danger. We agreed to watch out for each other and Terra.

For the first time in a long time, I didn't feel crazy. I felt like I was a part of something and a part of something big. Really big. Possibly, a world changer. I was relieved we weren't the chosen family. A scary thought crossed my mind. Z was a middle child.

At home, I placed the folded paper from the fountain cave in my treasure box—plenty of time to look at it tomorrow.

Terra jumped on my bed early the next morning. "Did ya hear?
"

I yawned and rolled over. "What?"

194

She jumped some more. "The Starres are moving back across the street."

I flew to the window. It looked as if the renters were leaving.

I turned back around to Terra. "Are the renters taking their kids out of school early?"

Terra plopped hard down beside me. "Yes, I think so. They're kinda young. Probably doesn't matter much."

I stared at her. "Who told you the Starres were coming back?"

She shifted her legs on my bed. "I think the neighbor renter told Mom. Said they were coming back next school year."

My face dropped. "Next school year? Are all of them coming back?"

"No." Terra looked like she was trying to remember. "I think the middle boy—the one you liked—is getting married or something."

Knife.

Stab!

Stab!

I lost interest right away. Who cared if Stella and Neb came back? Neb was a senior going to college. So Stella was coming back— big deal!

Terra jumped off my bed. "Anyway just thought you'd want to know."

What had started out as a great weekend had just hit a rocky place. I thought about the good things that had happened yesterday. I found the fountain. Jorden, Blue, and I talked about our common enemy. We'd figure it all out. One thing I knew— the Skyes were strong by ourselves—but we were stronger together.

"Last two weeks of school." Kelly announced as we all sat down for lunch.

I said to the group. "I'm going to enjoy them."

That's why when Heath asked me out Friday night I said yes and when Stone asked me out Saturday night I also said yes. I had two dates with two different guys in the same weekend. What a social butterfly I was!

I decided not to clue Grandma in on the book we'd found, but I asked her and she'd agreed to give Jorden lessons.

Wednesday of that week, I sat in my biology class working on my final when I heard two boys in another building having a conversation.

An unfamiliar voice said, "I read that Jorden is most afraid of snakes and Blue is most afraid of losing his girl Kate. We need to make that happen."

Another voice asked, "How do you know that?'

The first voice replied, "L.Bands showed me their essays from the beginning of the year. That's why we had them write about their fears so he could play on them."

L. Bands? Could it be Lava Bands?

I remembered we wrote about what we feared during the first week of school. I warned Jorden to look out for the snake. That afternoon Jorden found a snake in his locker.

Blue explained to Kate that someone was going to try to get her to break up with him. A false story about Blue cheating on her was gossiped about around school. Blue and Kate ignored it. Even when pictures were produced, Kate stood by Blue. She knew it wasn't true. She knew they were photo shopped or faked in some other way. Nothing could break them up.

Neither plan worked. With Blue, Jorden, and I working together, we could survive whatever the enemy threw at us.

Friday night arrived.

Heath showed up right on time. "You look wonderful, Leah. I thought we'd go to dinner and a movie. Okay?"

I nodded. We went to a Japanese place where they cooked the food right in front of you. The movie was really funny. I couldn't remember the last time I laughed that hard.

Heath walked me to my door. "I've never seen your room you know."

I opened the door. "You haven't? Mom and Dad are at a party

and the boys are out with their girls and Terra is at a spend the night. So come on in. "

We went in the den. I picked up a globe-themed beach ball lying on the floor. "Catch."

Heath had picked up a dart right at that time and threw it toward the dartboard. Perfect timing. It hit the beach ball and deflated it. "Sorry." Heath mumbled as he scooped up the deflated ball with the dart sticking in it.

He tossed the ball from hand to hand, as we headed to my room. "I like your room." He sat on the edge of the bed beside me.

He leaned in to kiss me. I backed off.

He looked a little hurt. "Are we ever going to kiss?"

I guessed I had better get that first kiss soon, but not tonight, not with two dates in two nights.

I smiled. "Soon."

"Another time, then. I can wait." He tossed the deflated ball at me. "Guess it's time to go, I'll show myself out."

I heard the door slam downstairs and I tossed the ball at the trash, but it missed. I walked over to retrieve it and try again when I noticed something strange. The dart had stabbed Florida right in Berry. I flipped the world beach ball over and the opposite side of the dart was Cairo, Egypt. It hit me, who did I know from Cairo? Patra!

My mind churned with an idea. I quickly printed a flat map of the world. I carefully dotted the five points—Berry; Alberta, Canada; Aleutian Islands; Alaska and Hawaii and drew the Island of the Star map first shared by Grandma Jewell. I cut that star out and laid it on the map matching Cairo and Berry— where did the other points go? I made marks at the United Kingdom, Northern Russia, Taiwan, Thailand, and Egypt. There it was—the opposite star. I knew Constance from England and Patra from Egypt were already here— that meant the next part of the prophecy was coming true. Some occurrences had already taken place: the eclipse, the developing gifts, the gathering of the Island of the Star clans and now the opposite star. The only thing left was the middle child of the chosen family to obtain the bloodstone.

That morning Mom brought a large package into my room. "This came for you early this morning. Special delivery."

I frowned. "Who's it from?"

She sat on the edge of my bed as I opened it. "Someone named Robert Lant."

I almost dropped it. A letter attached to the package read:

Dear Miss Leah Skye,

Mr. Robert Lant's last request was that we get his personal journal to you so we hired an investigator to find your address and make sure you got it.

It was signed by a lawyer and Mr. Lant's personal assistant.

I tore it open and out dropped a journal entitled "Island of the Star Clan." I didn't want to explain this to Mom. "Oh it's a book for a project I'm working on for school."

She started probing, "Who would assign a project this late in the year?"

I knew the only way to get her to leave me alone was to pull the spoiled brat card. "Grace, do I have to tell you every little thing that I do—get out of my business." It worked—she looked upset when she left. I felt bad.

I opened the journal. It seemed to be an account of what he'd learned about the clan. There were drawings and pictures of the serpent star tattoo. I slid it in my treasure chest to study later. Eerie, he must have decided to send it to me right before he had died. Why me? It looked personal. In my treasure box, I noticed the paper I'd taken from the fountain room. Unfolding one crease I read the notation. *To be opened only by the center child who possesses the bloodstone. Not me*—I thought and placed the note back in the treasure box and closed it. I'd discuss this with Blue and Jorden as soon as I could. I couldn't think about it now. Right now, I was late for school and I had a date to get ready for after that.

Stone arrived early. "Wanna go bowling?"

I smiled. "I'd love to. I haven't been bowling in years. "

At the local bowling alley, I beat Stone easily. He was a good sport and we bowled three games. Constance and some of her group were there making fun of the way people bowled. Maybe our opposite heritage could explain my intense hatred of her. Stone and I ate seafood afterwards.

This time, my house was full when Stone and I arrived after the date.

Stone walked me to my door. "Sounds like your family is having a party. I don't want to intrude. I'll go home now. I had a great time tonight." He cupped my hands. "You know, I *really* do like you."

"I know, I like you too."

He didn't even try to kiss me. He just held my hands tenderly. "Guess I'll go. Maybe another date next weekend?"

I hesitantly nodded. "Thanks, I really had a great time." And I meant it. "Maybe we will do it again sometime. We'll see."

I was standing on the porch watching him drive away when I heard the bushes move. "Who's there?"

Heath came out from behind a tree. "Leah, I had to tell you something. I couldn't wait another minute."

"What?"

He grabbed my hand and pulled me into the yard. "I love you."

I froze. I didn't know what to say. His eyes begged me to say it back, but I couldn't. I opened my mouth to speak with no idea what words would come out.

Suddenly the front door opened and my mom stood in the doorway. "Heath, is that you? What are you doing here?"

Heath let go of my hands. "Sorry, Mrs. Skye, I forgot to tell Leah something."

"Leah needs to come in now. She'll see you tomorrow. Okay, Heath?"

Heath mumbled. "It'll only take a minute. It's important."

Mom said firmly, "Not now, some other time. It's time for Leah to come in now."

Heath nodded and left. Mom and I went into the house.

Dad said, "We have news."

The whole family gathered in the living room.

"What?" Blue asked.

Mom giggled. "It's good news."

Dad grabbed Mom's hand. "Actually—-'

Mom blurted out. "This wasn't planned, but things happen sometimes and we hope you will be as happy as we are."

Jorden yawned. "Tell us already."

Dad beamed. "We're going to have a baby."

Blue's mouth, Jorden's mouth, and my mouth all dropped open simultaneously.

Terra squealed and hugged Mom. "Have a girl, I want a baby sister. I won't be the baby anymore. Yea!" She started dancing around the room.

Mom looked at us. "Well, at least one of them is happy."

We stole uncomfortable glances at each other and then hugged her. "Of course we're happy, just surprised."

Mom radiated.

I asked. "When?"

Dad said, "December—it's a Hawaiian baby."

Terra said. "Whatdya mean?"

Jorden threw his hands over his face. "Yuck, Dad."

Blue shook his head. "Too much information, Dad."

We all laughed and talked a bit more—mostly about where the baby would stay. Terra offered to share part of her room.

Dad hugged Mom. "I think an addition to the house is in order."

I could tell nothing was going to deter the two of them from being ecstatic about this whole "unexpected bombshell."

"I think it's great!" I forced out before I headed to my room.

Blue and I walked up the stairs together. He stopped on the steps as if he was having a revelation. "Leah if I'm number one, and Jorden's second, you're third, Terra fourth, and the new baby is fifth—

"He looked at me curiously. " —that makes you—"

I finished his sentence. "—the center."

He poked me with his finger. "You *are* now the middle child."

He stepped into his room as a pang of fear shot through me like a bullet. He was right—the final occurrence.

After dressing for bed, I felt brave and decided to open the paper from the fountain room. I sat in the middle of my bed, my hands trembling as I unfolded it. It consisted of two pages hand written by Gamma.

I'm not sure who will find this letter, but I write it in haste as I feel the end is near. After my husband died and when my son was young, I accidentally uncovered this hidden book, The Sky Clan Book. It documented the history of my husband's family. I studied the book and came upon a notation about two dates I was unable to decipher. I enlisted help from an expert Dr. Jake Milieu from North Carolina, who calculated the dates July 22, 2009 and December 21, 2010. This request resulted in my grandson, Nathaniel, meeting Dr. Milieu's daughter, Grace. They fell in love and married.

I gasped. Mom and Dad.

I researched Grace's family tree and discovered she was also a descendant of the ancient Sky clan. Their union has resulted in a son, Blue, and another child on the way. I invited Grace, Nathaniel, and her parents to visit our farm. I took Grace's parents to the fountain to divulge their heritage and share the book. I was unable to do either, as during the trip the most unthinkable event occurred. Before I had a chance to stop them they had both drunk from the fountain. Having studied the book, the only solution was for me to drink from the same cup. I know I will suffer the fatal consequence, but fear they will die younger than they should. It is out of love that I drank the liquid. My hope is that it will prolong their life. My daughter-in-law needs them.

I felt a sudden sense of sadness, as I realized that was why my grandmother and grandfather passed away so suddenly.

It is with a heavy heart and immense guilt that I state my intention to lock this book and all of this information in the fountain cave where I discovered it so many years ago. I hope the book finds its way to its rightful owner, the center child of the chosen family.

Groping to understand, I asked myself—Was I the center child?

I turned over the page and written in Old English calligraphy:

The Spirit Voice

The center child of the chosen family will be able to conjure the spirit to reveal the prophecy. The child must sit and hold the bloodstone in the right hand and repeat, "Take me on the spirit journey." If all is as it should be, secrets will be revealed.

I had to try. I placed the ruby in my right hand. I repeated, "Take me on the spirit journey," over and over.

In a few minutes, it seemed as if I had transcended and was floating on a cloud. Wisps were all around me and I felt light. I saw a winged angelic being.

"Spirit child, much unrest looms in your world. You will have to escape many dangers and survive great battles. Guard the bloodstone, it contains great power. Your powers have just begun to bloom. Be careful whom you trust. There is a betrayer. Beware of the serpent. Danger will emerge from places you don't suspect. Guard your gifts. The path you should take is..."

My trance seemed to be ending. Why? I needed the answer. What was my path? I heard my name. A familiar voice.

A delicious, mesmerizing smell consumed my room. The aroma took my breath away. My eyes focused on the shiny sun catcher Kelly had given me as it danced and twirled, with moonlight sending shards of light all around the room. I noticed my little treasure chest was open. The chocolate candy sat beside it. Who would do such a thing? Something shiny lay on the floor—my anklet. I squatted down between the bed and the window and reached for it.

An arm grabbed me and pulled me down. I let out a little scared yelp. Were my enemies here?

I slowly opened my eyes to face my attacker.

Chapter 38

"Z," I mumbled as I collapsed beside him out of sheer shock.

I heard his voice. "Leah, wake up!" I touched him—he was real.

He crawled out from under the bed and sat beside me on the floor.

I pinched myself. "Am I awake? How…"

Z talked. "It took me a week to get here." I had not heard his voice in over six months. Like elixir to my ears, it took my breath away.

"I waited six months for the supply plane. I stowed away on the plane and took a bus from Anchorage to Berry. It took forever. I've been in my house since morning waiting for you to be alone."

"I'm not dreaming. You're here. But I gave up on you. I moved on."

"I saw and heard." He snarled and hissed. "Do you love Heath now?" He searched my soul for what seemed like eternity as I defiantly held his stare.

I spat back. "Aren't you engaged? I thought you weren't coming back."

I'd transformed completely back into reality from the trance. Z was actually here. I could ask him all the things I'd bottled up for almost a year. A tear came down my cheek. I couldn't help it. I fought to keep it together. I hated him. "Are you engaged?"

He held his breath. "It's not what you think."

I couldn't imagine what he meant; what could I possibly think? "Either you're engaged or not." My anger boiled. "It's a simple yes or no answer!"

"I'm promised to a girl." He stared at me and I tried to look away before the hurt I felt registered.

His eyes pleaded as he spoke. "You don't understand the tribal ways. While I was there, a leader from the Aleutian Island tribe made a pact with my father for me to marry his daughter. "

"Arranged a marriage?" I stared at him with only rage. "...for you."

He nodded.

I glared at him, fury swelling. "Well, when's the wedding?"

"Never met her." He averted his eyes. "I can't marry her because..."

He stopped silent, but I heard his second voice. "I'm in love with you."

I melted a little.

He turned red with fury. "What about Heath, huh? Or Stone?"

"Heath's been here for me. He's important. Stone's a good guy." I shook. "I'm not sure I can ever forgive you."

He wiped the tear gently off my face. "Do you love either of them, Leah?"

I knew I had to tell the truth. "I love them both on some level. I can't lie about that."

His touch was so tender. My emotions were on fire. I hated him. No—I wanted to hate him. I wanted to with my entire self, but somehow my core—the real me, the deep down me—couldn't hate Z because Z was the best part of me. I knew that. I'd always known that. He was here now and a tranquil sense of joy engulfed me. I couldn't let him destroy any more of me and I knew that he could. I had to protect myself.

We sat on the floor, his warm arm barely touching mine.

He tried to explain. "My grandfather passed the day of your birthday."

"Sorry." I mumbled, feeling small.

"For more than a month great ceremonies were held in the village. My grandfather was a great man. It was because of his death that everything happened. During this time, a medicine man from the

Aleutian Village came and talked to my father. With no patriarch in place, an arranged marriage pact between his daughter, an Aleutian Princess, and me was struck by her father and our eldest member. The deal would ensure our tribe would be kept intact. Otherwise, our tribe would have to join with his, losing our history and identity. No one wanted that. I felt I had no choice. The medicine man had the mark—the star tattoo. The star tattoo symbolizes power."

I remembered the trance. Danger from places I didn't suspect. "Why you?"

Z frowned. "Not sure."

"Could he sense your gifts?" I couldn't stop staring at him.

"It's possible." He looked into my eyes. "All I know is I'm not going to marry her, arranged marriage or not."

I felt a peace I had not felt in a very long time.

The intense pain I'd endured during his absence eased a little. As dawn approached, he stood by the bed. The morning window light illuminated his face. Standing there, I saw how much he'd matured. He had been a boy the last time I had seen him. He had gotten taller and wider—wider in a good way. I wondered what he thought when he looked at me. I didn't know if my stirrings for him made him irresistible. I desperately didn't want to feel anything for him.

"I need to go."

I had to admit I didn't want him to leave. "Are you going to come back?"

"Yes." He leapt out onto the branch and I watched him creep back across the street.

Knowing he was over there would make my day harder and better at the same time. At breakfast the food tasted a little better, the conversation seemed a little livelier.

Mom noticed my behavior change. "Good date?"

I nodded and lied. "I'm excited about the new baby."

Mom stuffed back most of the joyful yelp.

Stone and Heath called that day; I talked to each of them all the while thinking about Z.

That night, the window opened and Z came in. My heart skipped a couple of beats.

"You're here." I gestured at two pillows and a blanket already arranged in our secret place on the floor between the bed and the window.

He sat down. His finger touched the tips of my fingers. "I enjoyed watching you and your family come and go today."

I wrinkled my nose. "Really? Must have been a boring day for you. Are you hungry?"

He touched my fingers again and smiled. "Hungry for you."

I had to keep my emotions in check. I felt the tingle of his touch and it sent shivers down my being. "What about your tribal rules?"

He shrugged. "Any rules that keep me from you have to be broken."

I struggled to protect my heart.

"What do you want for your future?" He asked, "What do you want to be—?"

I finished his thought. "...when I grow up?"

He shrugged. "Sounds silly, but I guess that is my question. We never talked about it."

I answered, "I've always wanted to be a doctor. I see myself curing some horrible disease or discovering a new way to operate."

"I believe you could make that happen. You're special, Leah. I've always felt it."

"And you?" I asked.

"Me? I thought about being a doctor too or a lawyer and return to Alaska to help my people. I haven't really made up my mind." He touched my chin. "Plenty of time for that."

The night was magical—no prophecy—no serpent star tattoos—just Z and me starting over.

Dawn approached. "I've got school tomorrow." I frowned.

"I know." He crouched on my window ledge. "I need to hide as long as I can. Can we meet somewhere this afternoon?"

"Maybe the lake? There's a secluded area I found quite by accident. Here, I'll show you." I got a piece of paper and drew him a map. "I'll make up some excuse...library...studying finals or something like that."

When he left, I felt empty.

I blew Heath and Stone off with lies about studying for finals. Kelly and Jane were a bit more trouble, but I succeeded by telling them my mom needed me around because of the surprise pregnancy.

I met Z that afternoon at the lake. We talked about what had happened the past year. He had been forbidden to see me since he had been promised to the Aleutian princess.

We stretched out on a blanket for a long while, not saying anything. It was strange how I could be near Z and it could fulfill me so much with no touching or talking.

That night he told me more. "My family's being banished from our adopted Alaskan tribe."

"Why?"

"For not following the old ways and not being loyal. Sorry, it's not the marriage thing. That seems to be a done deal." He shrugged. "I'm not sure why. Why couldn't it be Neb? He needs help finding a girl." We both laughed.

He told me about the parts of Alaska he missed. His family planned to return to Berry in the fall and Z guessed it might be sooner once they figured out where he was.

He touched my forehead after deciding to leave. "Get some sleep in the afternoon. Take a nap. Replenish yourself. I'll see you tomorrow night."

I watched him disappear into the night.

Z showed up late the next night. And I told him all about the attempts on Blue and Jorden, the lessons, the fountain, and the ruby. He listened intently as he held my hand.

I told him all about Stone and Heath. I didn't leave anything out. He didn't like it. We hugged gently most of that night. Before he left, he took my ankle, pulled it to him, and put the anklet on my foot. I made no move to stop him. I didn't want to stop him.

He left and as soon as he left, I wanted him back.

The next night we talked about Hawaii and what had happened there and about the gala and what had happened there. All the while, I drank in his aroma, his touch, all that was Z. With Z here, I was getting stronger. My gifts were growing more powerful each day. Z's gifts were growing too.

I told him about my and Jorden's connection. "I need to tell you a few other things. I have had a spirit voice journey." I told him all about the journey and the folded paper and the serpent tattoo.

He listened. "I need to tell you about my promised wife." He sounded defeated. "Her and her father are supposed to come with my parents in the fall. They might come sooner when they find out where I am."

"We don't know if he is good or bad." I trembled and he held me. It was getting harder to let him go. As the last darkness disappeared, Z vanished back to his house.

The whole last week of school was abuzz about graduation Saturday night. The ceremony was taking place in the town's civic center. Kate and Blue prepared all week.

All I could think of was seeing Z.

Friday night, we sat on the floor in each other's arms. I told him more about the gift lessons and that Jorden would get lessons starting this summer. I told him everything I knew about the prophecy, the book, and the legend. I couldn't think of anything else to tell him.

I didn't want him to leave. He caressed my face. I could hear his second voice. "I want to kiss you."

He pulled me close and his lips touched mine ever so gently as if I was a breakable doll. My desire for him was overwhelming. A missing part of me was suddenly, completely, and miraculously back again.

I had dreamed what my first kiss would be like. I'd seen movies. Some people almost devour each other. Others kiss hard. I didn't know what to expect, as I'd never been kissed.

I made no move to stop him. I couldn't. I wouldn't.

"You're so soft." He touched me and kissed my eyes, my cheeks, and my neck. He came back to my lips and kissed them again. He kissed my lips and my soul at the same time. It was consuming and exhilarating. It felt genuinely right.

My first kiss was everything I had hoped for. It was exquisite and divine.

I looked at his glowing eyes brimming full of love for me. I knew right then that Z was my one—the one that I was meant to be with. We would break the rules. We would chase our forbidden love. We were supposed to be. I had no doubt I was hopelessly and completely in love with him and no matter what happened, I would always be his and he would be mine. I knew we made claim on each other and our souls on that bedroom floor right there and then. And we sealed it with a cherished kiss of adoration.

I don't know how long we held each other. It was way into the night. Neither one of us wanted to let go.

He asked me before he left, "What are we going to do?"

"There's only one thing to do." I grabbed his hand. "We have to make a stand."

"Nobody even knows I'm here." He stared at me. "The prophecy?"

I clutched his hand and squeezed. "We have to be strong. We are the Starre and the Skye. We are the dreamers. We are the shakers and the movers. We make things happen."

I kissed him again passionately and without reserve.

He looked at me. "I love you Leah. It's always been you and it will always be you. You are *My One*."

I quivered from my spine down to my toes with excitement. "I know. I love you too." And I meant it.

That night as we walked into the Graduation Hall to let it be known that we were together and together forever no matter what kind of arranged marriages there were, my heart was full of joy.

I stood outside the door, happy. Everyone, our families, our friends, Heath, Stone, and the Aleutian Princess would have to understand. We would crack the secrets of the prophecy and discover what our roles were in that prophecy. We would find our nemesis and fight together. Our gifts would grow more powerful. Z and I had each other. We were stronger together. Forbidden or not.

Hand in hand, we opened the door and walked through to a graduation and our destiny.

Epilogue

It's been a week since Z and I walked into the graduation ceremony together. Most people weren't happy with Z's reappearance because of how much pain he'd caused me. I couldn't disagree. But I couldn't do without Z.

My parents balked. Z's parents were called.

A few days later, Mom poured me a glass of orange juice. "You ready for your first day at the hospital?"

Jorden pointed out the kitchen bay window. "Who's that over at the Starre's house?"

A tall, lanky older man got out of a cab and walked to the Starre's door.

I said, "I'll go over and find out."

Mom grabbed a basket of sweet rolls. "I'll come with you. Z's on punishment because of you. You aren't supposed to see him."

I knew.

We walked to Z's door and Mom knocked. "I brought sweet rolls for your visitor."

Mrs. Starre smoothed her hair. "Thanks. Come in."

We sat in the living room.

"Mrs. Skye and Leah, this is Ryan Thundersky."

I noticed the serpent star tattoo. Mother shook his hand, but his gaze settled on me.

He asked, "Will you walk with an old man, Leah?"

Curious, I nodded and we walked outside.

We sat on a bench and he said, "The ruby."

I grabbed my ruby. "What about it?"

Ryan Thundersky touched my shoulder and my ruby vibrated.

"Leah," Z walked out to the yard and I jerked around as Ryan Thundersky's hand fell from my shoulder.

Ryan Thundersky stood. "Z, I'm buying a house on the lake. I have come to finalize the plans. My daughter will be joining me in a month."

I glared at Z.

That night, I waited for the bay window to open. "What took you so long?"

Z crawled to our familiar place between the window and the bed. "I had a hard time getting out tonight."

I propped my head on my hand. "Ryan Thundersky's daughter is the one you're supposed to marry, right?"

Z touched my face. "I belong to you."

It was hard to think with him this close. He put his arm around my waist and pulled me to him. "I won't lose you again."

The scent of him filled my senses. His soft lips kissed my eyes.

I pulled back. "Z, we *have* to talk."

"Leah, I don't know anything. I'm forbidden to see you. I broke every tradition to come back to you. You are all that matters to me. Not Thundersky or his daughter."

I touched his face. "I'm sorry, Z."

He traced my lips. "Your boyfriends, Heath and Stone," I flinched and he pulled me closer. "—told me to stay away from you."

I locked eyes with him. "Nobody wants us to be together."

His hand encircled the back of my neck and we kissed. "We're getting good at this."

I sighed. "I love kissing you."

He stroked my hair. "I love you, Leah. Nothing will ever change that. I don't care who I'm promised to or if you have boyfriends trying to keep us apart or if we have clans and prophecies against us." He kissed me again. "I love you and that is all there is. Understand?"

Tears rolled out of my eyes. I buried my head in his chest so

213

overcome by emotion that I thought I'd explode.

I cried, "What are we going to do?"

"We'll figure it out together."

Somehow, I knew he was right. Things were different now. I knew that whatever happened, I wasn't in this alone anymore.

Other Books by Susan Larned Womble

1) **The Big Wheel** ISBN-13: 978-0-9913977-0-9
2) **Take The Helm** ISBN-13: 978-0-9913977-7-8
3) **Newt's World: Beginnings** ISBN: 978-0-9913977-1-6
4) **Newt's World: Internal Byte** ISBN: 978-0-9913977-2-3
5) **Newt's World: Beginnings Workbook Teacher's Edition** ISBN: 978-0-9913977-3-0
6) **Newt's World: Beginnings Workbook Student's Edition** ISBN: 978-0-9913977-4-7
7) **Newt's World: Internal Byte Workbook Teacher's Edition** ISBN: 978-0-9913977-5-4
8) **Newt's World: Internal Byte Workbook Student's Edition** ISBN: 978-0-9913977-6-1

Awards and Notables

- **Gold Medal Florida Book Award in children's literature 2008 for "Newt's World: Beginnings"**
- **Newt's World Beginnings on 2009, 2010, 2011, 2012, 2013, 2014 Just Read Florida Recommended Reading Lists**

ABOUT THE AUTHOR

Susan Womble is an award-winning author. Susan Womble lives in Tallahassee, Florida with her family. She is a retired National Board Certified teacher with a career of teaching grades K-12th in the areas of reading, special education, language arts, math, social studies, and the profoundly handicapped. Visit **www.susanwomble.com** for more information. Contact her at **susan.womble@gmail.com**

www.ingramcontent.com/pod-product-compliance
Lightning Source LLC
Chambersburg PA
CBHW070625130626
46556CB00001B/473